MW01593946

HIGH CONTRAST

A Collection of Tales

Ian Thomas Healy

Local Hero Press Edition

High Contrast: A Collection of Tales
Published by Local Hero Press, LLC

1st Printing
Local Hero Press: trade paperback, October 1, 2016
Printed in the United States of America

All rights reserved worldwide
Copyright © 2016 Ian Thomas Healy
http://www.ianthealy.com

ISBN: 1539077667
ISBN-13: 978-1539077664

Cover art by Local Hero Press, LLC
Sources: 1. "Power farming displaces tenants from the land in the
western dry cotton area. Childress County, Texas Panhandle", June
1938, Dorothea Lange [Public domain], via Wikimedia Commons
2. Bird images via Obsidian Dawn, www.obsidiandawn.com.
Book design by Local Hero Press, LLC

This is a work of fiction. Names, characters, places, and incidents are
either the product of the author's imagination or used fictitiously.
Any resemblance to actual events, locales, or persons, living or
dead, is entirely coincidental.

This book, its contents, and its characters are the sole property of
Ian Thomas Healy. No part of this publication may be reproduced,
stored in or introduced into a retrieval system, or transmitted in any
form or by any means (electronic, mechanical, photocopying,
recording, or otherwise) without written, express permission from
the author. To do so without permission is punishable by law. Please
purchase only authorized electronic editions, and do not participate
in or encourage electronic piracy of copyrighted materials. Your
support of the author's rights is appreciated.

Books by Local Hero Press

The *Just Cause Universe*

Just Cause
The Archmage
Day of the Destroyer
Deep Six
Jackrabbit
Champion
Castles
The Lion and the Five Deadly Serpents
Tusks
The Neighborhood Watch
Arena (Winter 2017)
JCU Omnibus, Vol. 1
JCU Omnibus, Vol. 2
The Bulletproof Badge

Collections

The Good Fight
The Good Fight 2: Villains
Muddy Creek Tales
Caped
High Contrast

The Pariah of Verigo

Pariah's Moon
Pariah's War

Other Novels

Assassin
Blood on the Ice
Hope and Undead Elvis
Making the Cut
Rooftops
Space Sharks
Starf*cker
The Guitarist
The Milkman
The Oilman's Daughter (with Allison M. Dickson)
Troubleshooters

Nonfiction

Action! Writing Better Action Using Cinematic Techniques

Table of Contents

Bread and Circuses

Tending bar is one of those jobs that's at the same time more glamorous than movies and less exciting than watching paint dry. I've seen my fair share of bizarre and exciting incidents within the confines of Wilbur's in the five years I've worked there. Still, it's only a small neighborhood bar in a gentrified part of town, and the regulars are slowly dying off one by one. There have been days where not a single person walks through the door with its frosted glass and I've spent entire shifts playing the online trivia game that the owner installed as a hook for the younger, hipper crowd. I'm still not sure why he hasn't shuttered the bar. I don't know how he affords to pay his staff, but the checks always clear.

I drew the short stick to work the unpopular closing shift on the Fourth of July, and it looked like it would be yet another shift sans customers. Nevertheless, I filled my ice cabinet and topped off the peanuts in the bar dishes, just in case. It never hurts to be professional. I had high hopes that business would pick up after the city finished lighting off its fireworks display but until then it figured to be several hours of quiet and online trivia.

So when the door tinkled open, I was surprised enough that I forgot to answer the trivia question and the timer ticked down to zero. The customer walked in—a man in his late thirties or early forties, unshaven, wearing cargo shorts, a t-shirt, and a military fatigues jacket. He plopped himself down at the bar, never once making eye contact with me. He looked like one of the homeless guys who lurked around the park on the next block, holding up a signs that said *will work for food god bless*. I glanced toward the phone at the end of the counter, just to remind myself it was still there. The guy didn't look like he was there to start any trouble, but it didn't hurt to be sure. He looked like he'd been through hell and back, though, and with his military jacket, I wondered if he might be a veteran. I knew fireworks could be a problem for guys with PTSD, and maybe he'd come into the bar to find some peace and quiet from the noise and crowds outside.

Nevertheless, he was a customer, and this was my job, so I set aside the trivia controller. I wrangled my face into my best smile, and stepped over to him, setting a paper napkin down before him. "Evening, sir. What can I get for you?"

"Beer."

There are about a million responses to this one, most of which you learn your first week in bartending school. Most of them are designed to make the customer laugh and loosen up, but this guy didn't carry himself like he was looking for a laugh. His very presence seemed like a soporific. I found myself speaking barely louder than a whisper. "Sure. What kind do you prefer?"

"Whatever's room temperature."

He had an odd accent, and coupled with his request for warm beer, I figured he was from out of the country.

I opened a bottle of the Irish ale we kept in the cabinet at the vendor's request and poured it into a mug, watching the man out of the corner of my eye. Numerous scars decorated a face that might once have been handsome before encountering whatever had done all that damage. I glanced downward and saw his hands were similarly scarred. Definitely a veteran, then. Those kinds of scars only came from shrapnel or bullets. I wondered if I should thank him for his service, but somehow it didn't seem appropriate. He still looked homeless, and I was leery about getting close enough to accidentally smell him. The stench of some of those people was enough to kill an entire day's worth of appetite.

"Six dollars." I set the mug on the napkin.

He produced a ten dollar bill from a thick money clip. "Keep it."

All right, so he wasn't homeless then. "Thanks, mister. My name's Carl. Let me know if you need anything else. Just try not to monopolize my time."

At that, the man raised his head enough to look up and down the bar. A wry smile crossed his face at the lack of other customers. "I'll be good."

I took out a rag and wiped down a spot on the bar that was already clean. "Not going to watch the fireworks tonight?"

"No, I don't much like them." He took a long sip of his beer and then fixed his gaze on me. His eyes belonged on someone much older, someone who'd seen far more suffering and death than anyone should in a lifetime. I actually took a step backward.

I decided to risk the question. "Are you a veteran?"

The man lowered his head and chuckled into his beer. "Thanks, kid. Best laugh I've had in a long time."

My ears burned at the *kid* comment. I wasn't that much younger than him. "Boy, if that's the best laugh you've had, I'd say you're overdue for some more."

The man took a long drink from his mug. "I'm Eric," he said. "Or Erik, Erich, Elrik, Uruk, Erikku, Erico, or Eirikr. Or a hundred other names. But right now I'm Eric. And yes, I'm a veteran."

"Iraq? Afghanistan? Somewhere in the Middle East?"

"Yes. Iraq or Afghanistan or somewhere in the Middle East. Most recently, anyway."

"Did you, uh, get those scars there?" I winced as I said it. I sounded like a small-town rube, and it was a rude question to boot. If he'd have gotten up and left, I wouldn't have blamed him, and I'd have paid for his beer out of my own pocket for being an asshole.

It didn't seem to bother him. He shrugged in a noncommittal way. "No more than anywhere else. I've been a soldier for a long time."

"Oh?" I poured myself a beer. It was a holiday and I certainly wasn't going to see the boss today—not when he could be off barbecuing and boozing with his family and friends. "How long?"

Eric set down his beer and fixed me with that gaze again. "About seven thousand years, give or take a couple decades."

I laughed and nearly blew beer out my nose. I had to wipe my eyes with a towel. I set it down on the bar and poured him another beer. "This one's on me. You really had me there."

"I'm not joking." His voice was quiet in counterpoint to the muffled crowd noises out on the street.

"Sure you are." I chuckled and drank half my beer.

Without a word, he slid out of his fatigues jacket and let it fall to the floor. His arms were covered with a network of scars. I gasped. He pointed to several of them in sequence. "This one was a bullet in the Falklands. Shrapnel in Korea. Razor wire on Normandy Beach. Bayonet in Appomattox. Tomahawk in Dakota Territory. Oh, and this one was from a Legionnaire's spear." He continued, using names and places I'd never heard before.

"You're making fun of me," I said, the protest sounding weak in the quiet of the bar.

"Am I?" he replied. He pulled down the neck of his t-shirt to show a larger ragged scar along the base of his throat. "Self-inflicted, Kadesh, 1281 BC." He showed me several circular scars on his temples. "Self-inflicted,

4

Milan, 1508. Self-inflicted, Chicago, 1871. Self-inflicted, Leningrad, 1914. Shall I go on?"

"Mister, I think maybe you ought to leave," I said, and meant it. The guy was creeping me out.

"As I said, I've been a soldier for seven thousand years. It's all I'm good at. I can't die, although God knows I've tried just about every way possible. Watch." He grabbed my bar towel, set his hand on it. His other hand flashed around in a blur of motion, something sharp and shiny held in it. With a resounding thunk, he drove a switchblade all the way through the back of his hand into the bar surface.

I yelled in surprise and lunged for the bar phone. "Stop." His quiet word brought me up short like it had been a shouted command. He regarded the knife protruding from his hand sadly and took a sip from his beer. He pulled the knife out, folded it, and tucked it back into the pocket from which it came.

A small spot of blood decorated the white towel. He held up his hand and I watched as the wound closed, leaving a fresh scar amid the others.

"You're serious?" I whispered.

He nodded. "I was born in Sumeria some seven thousand years ago. I don't know why I stopped aging and started healing. I began as a soldier and since then it's all I've been. There's always another war to fight, always another conflict. It's what men do best." He raised his glass in a toast.

"We're not really that bad, are we?"

"Kid, I've seen atrocities that would make your toes curl. I've *done* things that bad. I've seen the worst Man has to offer." He smiled suddenly. "Hell, I *am* the worst Man has to offer. You know how many men I've killed? I can't begin to count them. And women. And children." He finished his second beer. "So to answer your original question, I don't like fireworks because I don't like being reminded of what they represent."

"Well, they always represented freedom to me. The celebration of our independence."

"I know. I fought for it. First with the French. Then with Washington's troops. Stupid. Your empire will fall like all the others. I'm amazed it's lasted this long."

"If you thought it was so stupid, why fight for it?"

He shrugged. "Seemed like a good idea at the time. I guess I had higher hopes for your country. Franklin, Jefferson, Washington. They were sharp guys. Idealists. They had a plan to build something different, something that had never existed in the world before. And you all turned it into bread and circuses."

"Excuse me?"

"Juvenal. He was a Roman poet. Liked boys with curly hair and girls with dark skin. Drank too much wine. Commented that the people gave up all their power so long as the government gave them bread to eat and circuses to entertain. Not really any different than today."

I blushed. I was DVRing a marathon of *Ancient Aliens* at home and had intended to binge-watch it over a pair of large pizzas during the next couple of days. I was guilty of exactly what he'd said.

"Why are you here at all? I mean here, now, in this bar?" I asked him at last.

Eric looked at me. "I was just passing through and wanted a drink. I left Syria a year ago and I've been wandering since. Things are different now. War is different. I'm not sure how to fight it now. I can't tell which is the right side anymore."

"Well . . . our side is, isn't it?"

He fixed me with that gaze again. "Is it?"

I opened my mouth to reply, but couldn't find the words. Anything I'd have said would have felt hollow.

He set another ten on the bar. "Thanks for the drinks, Carl. Enjoy your Independence Day, such as it is. But ask yourself . . . are you really free?"

And just like that, he left the bar and I never saw him again.

I don't watch TV anymore. Maybe Eric's war isn't mine, but I can see the signs in daily life everywhere. We're not free, not really.

Not anymore.

Dental Plan

Robert's first tooth fell out into his bowl of minestrone soup at Spagnoli's while he was discussing trade tariffs with a client. It didn't even hurt at first. He opened his mouth to argue a point about China and the tooth just plunked right down into the broth, followed by a droplet of blood that swirled like a dash of pepper sauce.

Then the acidity of the tomatoes hit him and he winced as he raised a napkin to his mouth. "Ow! What the hell?"

"What's the matter, Bob? Bite your tongue?" Steven, his lunch companion, ate another forkful of his Caesar salad, just like the prissy little bastard he was. Salad was only fit for rabbits. Maybe the minestrone didn't have any meat in it, but it was a damn sight more substantial than weeds.

"My tooth! My damn tooth just fell out!" He pushed his chair back from the table. "I'll be right back." He hurried to the bathroom.

Sure enough, there it was: a bloody hole in his otherwise pristine, chemically-whitened smile. It was the one right behind his upper right canine. What was that called? The cuspid? Robert didn't know and didn't care. All he knew was his tooth had fallen out and if he could figure out how to sue somebody over it, he would.

He crammed a wad of paper towels in the gap to stem the bleeding and returned to the table.

"Everything all right, Bob?" Steven asked. He already had his entrée and was digging into a large portion of lasagne. Vegetarian, of course.

Bob's sausage-and-peppers had been delivered as well. The soup remained, set off to one side. His tooth still poked out of the slowly-congealing broth. It made him feel queasy looking at it. "No, I'm not okay. I lost a tooth."

"Cool story, bro. Got a good dental plan?"

"Hell yes I do." It wasn't just a Cadillac of dental plans; it was a Ferrari. He had quarterly cleaning and bleaching appointments. He had sealant treatments, fluoride treatments, any treatments he could possibly ever need or want. In his line of business, when millions of dollars were on the line with every negotiation, nothing tilted the odds in his favor like a perfectly straight set of pearly whites. It amused him to no end that something so simple could be so intimidating to the opposition. Robert texted his secretary to cancel his afternoon schedule and to get him an emergency visit to his dentist.

"Are you finished with your soup, sir?" asked the waitress, who had an ass he'd normally appreciate.

For one perverse moment, Robert almost reached down to fish out his lost tooth. What would he even have done with it if he had? It's not like the dentist could reattach the damn thing. Lost is lost. He shook his head. "Yes, I'm done."

The rest of the meal passed by in a blur for him. He only sort of paid attention to Steven's points about why they should move the manufacturing base to South America. Robert spent most of the time exploring the new, unfamiliar hole in his mouth and coppery tang of blood coming out of it. It felt like there was a raw nerve exposed and it stung every time he touched it. Even so, he couldn't stop.

The end of the business lunch was a relief. Robert shook Steven's hand and promised to be in touch. Then he flagged down the first cab he saw outside the restaurant and gave the address of his dentist.

By the time the cabbie dropped him at the dentist's office building, the tooth socket had stopped bleeding and wasn't even hurting very much. Robert kept feeling it up with his tongue. He hoped the dentist could put in an implant, maybe even a partial if it came to it.

The office lobby was full of MILFs and their snot-nosed kids. Any other day, Robert would have made a play for one of them. Most women with kids were either single, or sex-starved soccer moms looking for some excitement in their lives. But the missing tooth was a real confidence killer. *Maybe some other time, ladies*, he thought.

All the sports and car magazines were six months out of date, but Robert paged through a *Car and Driver* anyway, not really reading or even looking at the pictures.

He jumped when the hygienist pushed open the door from the back rooms and called his name. He forced his tongue away from the hole and followed the cute redhead back to an examination room.

The chair was comfortable, unlike the tortuous ones he remembered from his childhood. He'd even fallen asleep during cleanings before. "What seems to be the trouble, Robert?" she asked, perky and cheerful beyond all reasonable expectations.

"I lost a tooth."

"That's not good. Let's take a look." She poked and prodded around in his mouth for a few minutes before sitting back and raising her clear safety glasses onto her forehead. "Looks like it was a fairly clean break. The root just let go. We shouldn't have any problem fitting you with a prosthetic."

The dentist joined them in a couple of minutes and performed his own examination. With his carefully-coiffed silvered hair and manicured nails, he looked far more like he should have been in a commercial espousing the benefits of a particular brand of toothpaste. After some poking and prodding, he agreed with the hygienist's analysis. "No evidence of decay, not even a speck of plaque. You take good care of your teeth. Did you bite into anything hard?"

"I was eating soup."

"Ah. Well, sometimes teeth just fall out."

"So there's nothing I did wrong? Nothing I can blame on anyone else?" Robert felt supremely disappointed that there was nobody he could sue.

The dentist laughed. "I'm afraid not. Nothing that would hold up in court, anyway. I think the best thing would be for you to sit still while I take some new molds. It'll take us a couple days to put together your prosthetic."

"What am I supposed to do in the meantime?" asked Robert.

"Avoid crunchy foods and practice the story you'll tell your friends," said the dentist.

They took molds of his mouth, using trays of pink goop that tasted slightly of mint but mostly of sand. He gagged when the hygienist slid the too-large trays into his mouth, and called her uncouth names under his breath when she took them out.

The dentist promised to have his prosthetic ready by Monday.

He headed for home. On the way, he called his secretary to tell her he'd be away from the office all day Friday and a good chunk of Monday. When she asked what she should tell the department manager, he said to say he was working from home. He had no intention of doing any such thing, but it was important to keep up appearances.

As Robert fumbled for his keys, his neighbor Mrs. Peavey opened her door and her yappy dog raced out to the end of his leash, barking at him like a furry machine gun. "Bijou! You stop that right now!" The elderly woman gave the leash a firm yank, making the chihuahua yelp. "I'm so sorry, Robert. He's been such a little devil today."

"That's all right, Mrs. Peavey." He wrestled his key into the lock.

"What are you doing home so early?"

He winced. Mrs. Peavey was a lonely spinster who made the lives of everyone in the building her business. He'd helped her with her groceries one day when he'd felt like he needed some good karma, and in return, she'd decided they were best buds. "I'm, uh, I'm sick," he said. "Probably contagious."

The old biddy's wrinkled face fell. "Oh, that's terrible! I'll make some soup and bring it over later."

More soup. That's all he needed. "You don't have to do that." Robert planned to get a bottle of Jack Daniels inside him before too long.

"Nonsense," she said. "I insist. I won't stay and chat, I promise. I don't want to catch whatever you've got. But you live alone, and someone's got to look after you. Lord knows none of those girls you bring home are worth anything."

Robert repressed a sigh. He wasn't going to be able to get rid of her. "Thanks, Mrs. Peavey."

"Come along, Bijou." The tiny dog growled once more at Robert before dutifully following his mistress out the building door.

Stupid rat dog. Given five minutes alone with the beast, Robert was reasonably certain he could dropkick it into the next county. He went into his apartment and locked the door behind him.

Two hours later, he'd changed into sweats and a t-shirt, and true to his plan, he started drinking enough Jack and Coke to make his vision blur. Naturally enough, his drinking eventually led to hunger. Living the life of a bachelor who preferred dining out to cooking meant he didn't have much food in the apartment. An examination of his preferred delivery services revealed nothing that sounded the least bit appetizing.

A knock upon his door gave him pause and broke him out of his contemplation of food. Who would be stopping by unannounced? Surely, nobody knew he was at home. At first he feared it was some girl, angry at him for not using a condom and displaying a furious pregnant belly.

He went and hid in his closet.

The knock was repeated once more and eventually it penetrated his alcoholic haze that it must have been Mrs. Peavey with her promised soup. Soup didn't sound particularly appetizing, but at least it was easy to get without having to deal with a delivery guy. He staggered to the door and opened it. A plastic container sat on his plain welcome mat with a handwritten note on a yellow post-it. *Get well soon!*

Robert retrieved the soup and set it on his counter. He didn't bother with a bowl, just dug a spoon out of the dishwasher and opened the lid. The stench of chicken broth assaulted his senses like the reek of rotten meat in a city dumpster. His bathroom was too far away; he vomited into the kitchen sink. Everything he'd drank on his otherwise empty stomach came up in a burning glut, punctuated by the clink of something small and hard on the stainless steel.

Another tooth.

Ropy saliva dribbled down from Robert's lips. He stared at the errant tooth, his mind racing with panicky shock. "Wha' th' hell?" he mumbled through booze-numbed lips. Blood dripped into the acidic puddle in the sink. His tongue tripped over the fresh hole. It had been one of the front ones on the bottom.

He knew he should call the dentist. Sure, teeth sometimes just fell out, but not in groups. Something was wrong, though the alcohol was dulling the reality of it a bit. Before he could think on it too much longer, he lunged for the faucet handle and washed away the evidence of his oral failure.

He would call the dentist in the morning. Drunk was no way to contact a professional, even in a perceived emergency. He wasn't too inebriated to protect his reputation.

Robert went to bed, and that night he was plagued by nightmares that kept him tossing and turning. By the morning, he couldn't remember a single one, but he was ravenous.

He found two more teeth under his back at the base of his pillow.

"Christ," he mumbled. His mouth ached and it was full of the metallic taste of dry blood. What was that now, four teeth? He felt around with his tongue and sure enough, there were now four gaps. What the fuck? He staggered to his bathroom and examined his mouth in the mirror. Four fresh gaps marred his grimace. Anymore, and he'd probably have to be fit with a set of dentures. How was he going to close a deal with a mouthful of teeth like Mrs. Peavey's and breath reeking of Polydent? How would he be able to wow the college girls if he got drunk and the damn things came loose mid-sentence or mid-kiss? He felt like a creepy old man. "Christ," he said again, feeling the gaps with his fingers. He wondered if there was some kind of oral disease that could make teeth drop out.

His phone was on the charger by his bed. He turned around to retrieve it and call the dentist, and his stomach cramped up so hard that he fell to the bathroom floor, hunched over in a fetal position. "Oh shit!" he gasped. Hunger pangs assailed him like he hadn't eaten in days. Even with his missing teeth, all he could think about was to get something in his belly.

He plundered his kitchen but found nothing except Mrs. Peavey's soup from the night before, now congealed into a fatty, rancid mess.

He didn't care. He ate it.

The chicken had a distinctively bitter flavor and the gelid broth slid down his throat like sour gravy. The vegetables were unrecognizable mush. He finished it, wondering if he would lose another tooth. It wasn't as disturbing to him as it had been the day before. Indeed, it had almost become a point of curiosity. How far would it go? How many of his pearly whites would get washed down the drain?

He spent a few minutes exploring his mouth with his tongue. None of his other teeth felt loose. The gaps of his missing pearly whites were placed seemingly at random. His gums were sore and ragged.

He called the dentist's office. The receptionist said that his dentist was out of the office until Monday. "Is it an emergency?"

"Yes, it's a goddamn emergency!" shouted Robert. "I've lost four teeth. Four! I've spent thousands of dollars on my mouth at your office and now I've lost four teeth, you stupid cunt! Call him and tell him to get his ass off the links and back into the office to fix my fucking mouth!"

She hung up on him.

Robert flung his phone across the apartment where it shattered against his front door. "Sue them," he said. "I'll sue them right the fuck out of business." His stomach rumbled and twisted. Hunger made him feel shaky and light-headed, like his blood sugar was bottoming out. Mrs. Peavey's soup hadn't done more than take the edge off. He'd have to go out, get some real food.

"Maybe I pissed off the Tooth Fairy," he said aloud, and then broke into a fit of giggles. He ran back to his bedroom and shoved the teeth under his pillow. "That's two, you hear me? I better get fifty cents. It would be a dollar, but I already tossed the other two. My bad." He laughed like it was the best joke ever.

For the first time in years, Robert left his apartment without having showered. He wore a ratty Yankees cap, stubble dotting his face. He looked like the panhandlers he always saw on street corners with their cardboard signs. Maybe he should make one too. *Will lose teeth for money.* He chuckled about it until another tooth dropped out and tracked blood spots all the way down his front of his t-shirt, on its journey to the hallway carpet.

And then it wasn't funny anymore.

"Goddammit!" He shrieked in the solace of the hall. "What the fu—" Another tooth sailed out from between his lips. This one a front incisor. Blood ran down his chin like he'd been punched in the mouth.

He gagged on the taste of his blood and clamped his jaw tight to try to keep from vomiting. That mistake cost him one of his molars, and before he could do anything to stop it, the tooth rolled right down the back of his throat like an aspirin.

All pretenses at civility forgotten, Robert screamed in fear and disgust. Mrs. Peavey's day-old chicken soup splattered against the wall, mixed with blood to make a rancid, toothsome mess. No one peeked out of their doors at the scene. Maybe to avoid confronting the mad man who had suddenly invaded the building. All except Mrs. Peavey, that is.

Her door flew open and she was beside him in a moment. "Oh dear, you're still very sick. What were you thinking, trying to leave?" Bijou the dog yapped around Robert's ankles and growled at him.

He couldn't form words with his stinging mouth, instead mouthing the *help me.* Mrs. Peavey got her arms around him and helped him up. The frail looking woman was surprisingly strong. She brought him into her apartment and laid him down on her couch.

"Now you just stay right there and I'll get you a towel and a glass of water." She bustled off toward her kitchenette. Bijou leaped up onto a basket in a chair by the couch and rested his chin on the edge, glaring at him and growling anytime Robert looked at him.

Mrs. Peavey's apartment was much nicer than Robert's. Where his was simple and utilitarian, a place to keep his things and to sleep, hers felt like a home. Her furniture was clean and dusted, and all the wood was polished to a friendly sheen. She had pictures on the walls of people Robert assumed were her children and grandchildren, and several of herself with a man who must have been her husband before he died.

Robert's stomach rumbled so loud that Bijou snarled at him. He shot the dog a look of pure venomous hatred that didn't faze the animal one bit, but made him feel just a bit better. The tiny chihuahua was all skin and bone. Not even enough meat for an appetizer.

Where had *that* thought come from?

Before Robert could consider it further, Mrs. Peavey returned, her arms laden with a variety of cures and comforts. "Here," she said, burdening him with items as she named them. "The ice pack is for your head and the hot water bottle for your feet. Wrap yourself in this blanket. Don't worry about getting it dirty. I'll wash it later. In case you feel sick again, here's a waste basket."

Robert's stomach roiled as it tried to eat itself. He couldn't believe how hungry he felt, even after being sick. He began shivering, as if he had a high fever.

Mrs. Peavey noticed the shakes too, and pulled a glass thermometer from her bag. "You don't look well at all. Let's check your temperature."

Robert didn't have the strength to argue, even though he was desperately afraid to open his mouth again. Mrs. Peavey's gentle insistence forced it open, and another tooth dropped out to nestle in a fold of the blanket wrapped around him.

"Oh dear," said Mrs. Peavey as she plucked it from where it had fallen. "You just lost . . ." Then she really looked at Robert's open mouth and realized how many fresh gaps there were. "Robert, what on earth happened to you? You're missing half your teeth!"

He was on the verge of breaking up into hysterical laughter. Or hysterical tears. Or just general hysterics. "Only half?" he said in a trembling voice. "I'dsh have shought at leasht two-shirds by now." His voice had a strange lisp to it since all his front teeth were missing. It made his pronunciations odd.

The mania came over him like the tide washing in over jagged rocks. He was laughing and crying at the same time, as his remaining teeth rained down like hail, punctuated by splatters of blood and bile. His stomach cramped painfully and he hunched over, wanting to vomit, but he had nothing left to spit out.

Mrs. Peavey backed away from him, as if afraid that whatever was wrong with him might be contagious. Nevertheless, she took on an authoritative tone. "Robert, get a hold of yourself." Bijou leaped from his basket and pelted for the back bedroom, tail locked between his legs.

Robert gasped for breath, heart pounding. "I'm shorry, I'm shorry." He grabbed a glass of water and spilled half of it down his front trying to get it to his mouth, which was now shriveled and slack without the integrity of his teeth.

"Have you been to see a doctor?"

"I went to the dentisht yeshterday. Shey took moldsh. God, I shound sho shtrange."

Mrs. Peavey brightened a little. "Well, if they took molds, it should be simple for them to whip up some good dentures for you. I wear some myself." She made her top plate rattle in her mouth. "I bet you never knew."

To be fair, Robert wouldn't have noticed if she'd dyed her hair blue. He'd never paid much attention to women he didn't find sexually attractive. There was something about Mrs. Peavey, though, that he'd never noticed before. Something about her was desirable. He didn't know what it was, but he saw her in a new, almost delectable light. Never once had he been involved with a woman older than himself—not even the cougars who frequented some of the same bars he did. And Mrs. Peavey was old enough to be his grandmother. Nevertheless, he felt like he wanted to lose himself in her embrace. She had that peculiar old-lady smell that he'd always associated with his grandmother. It was a blend of flowers, Jurgen's lotion, and the tang of sweat on old skin beneath it all. His strange desire made the hunger pangs much more acute. He groaned. Another tooth broke free and he spat it into the water. He counted what was left with his tongue.

Nine.

How in the hell had he lost all but nine teeth in just under twenty-four hours? The word *cancer* made its way through his frightened brain and touched off a new crying jag. "I don't know what'sh wrong wish me."

Mrs. Peavey put her arms around him. "Shhh, it's going to be okay."

Robert let himself be comforted, suffering her ministrations in silence until his stomach growled so loudly that she pulled back. One of his teeth had caught in the weave of her sweater and he couldn't help but stare at it, a tiny ivory nugget with crimson highlights. Make that eight, now.

"My goodness, is that your tummy rumbling so loud?" she asked.

"Yesh," said Robert. "I'm sho hungry. It'sh all I can shink about. But I don't know what I can eat wishout my teesh."

"I'd be happy to make you some more soup. I can blend it so it'll be smooth enough that you can drink it. Would you like that?"

Robert nodded. It actually didn't sound the least bit appetizing, but he was desperate for food. He couldn't remember ever being so hungry. The thought of sustenance was almost erotic the way it caressed his mind. He didn't even know what he craved, but anything would be better than starving to death in a puddle of tooth-filled bile.

"I've got chicken thawed, but I'll have to run to the store to get fresh vegetables for the broth." She smiled. "That's the secret to good soup. You're welcome to stay here while I'm gone. Unless . . . Are you allergic to dogs?"

Robert was about to say he was, but when she'd said she had thawed chicken, saliva flooded his mouth with such force that it popped another tooth loose. Not wanting to look gauche, he swallowed it. It scratched his throat going down, but his stomach didn't instantly reject it. "No, I'm fine wish dogsh."

Mrs. Peavey gathered up her coat, keys, and purse. "I shouldn't be gone that long. I wrote my cell phone number in the kitchen. If you need to, don't hesitate to call me. And if you get worse, for God's sake, call nine-one-one."

"I will, and Mrsh. Peavey? Shanksh."

She smiled, making crow's feet wrinkles. "You're welcome, Robert. And please, call me Trudy. Feel free to use or eat whatever you need while you're here."

"Shrudy," he said. "I will. See you lasher."

She left and he threw off the blanket. His shivering and hysterics had vanished, leaving only that gaping hole in his belly that screamed to be filled. His tongue worked against his remaining teeth, wiggling each one loose in turn. As each one broke free, he spat it across the apartment like an elementary school kid with paper spitwads.

By the time he reached the kitchen, his mouth was barren and tasted of blood. His jaw felt funny, too, like he needed to yawn but couldn't. He ran his tongue over his naked gums. They felt soft and spongy, and he wondered how he was going to eat anything. Even his tongue felt odd—thicker than normal, like it was swollen, and the tip was really sore and felt hard against his gums.

The chicken sat on the counter in a styrofoam tray, wrapped in plastic. Robert's stomach wrenched when he saw it. He realized that he had no idea how to cook it, or how he'd eat it without teeth. "Ah well, how harth can ith be?" His voice sounded odd, ringing in his ears like it came out of a busted stereo speaker—buzzy and distorted.

Drool ran unhindered from his bottom lip as he stuck a finger onto the wrap and slit open the package with his fingernail. His entire mouth ached as the mild, sulfur smell of the room-temperature chicken filled his head. His tongue ran over swellings that lined his gums, insides of his cheeks, and roof of his mouth. It was like some kind of allergic reaction, except it felt good, despite the pain.

Robert took one of the thighs from the package and held it up to his mouth, mindless of the potential for disease. He answered only to his hunger now. His tongue split apart, leaving something sharp and raspy like a metal file in its place. He closed his eyes and shoved the chicken against his lips. They locked into the meat like a suction cup. Barbs like cat claws emerged from every part of his mouth to penetrate the meat and hold it in place. His tongue flailed against the flesh, shredding it as efficiently as an industrial blender. Juicy muscle tissue and spongy cartilage flowed down his throat into his belly, where his body attacked it with the fervor of a thousand starving men.

Within seconds, he stripped all the meat from the bones and threw the ragged scraps into the sink. He dove into the package for another piece and then another. It tasted wonderful, like bacon and brownies and Guinness all together. He polished off the rest of the chicken in short order and wiped his hands down the front of his shirt.

The enormity of his feast should have shocked him, but he was still hungry. Some part of him railed at this metamorphosis, but he could barely hear it. His conscience might as well have been calling all the way from the North Pole with nothing more than a tin can attached to a string. His new brain, instinctual and reptilian, was the one in charge now, and it was focused on only one thing: food. Only, he needed something warm this time. Preferably something freshly dead. He turned away from the kitchen and padded across the apartment toward Mrs. Peavey's bedroom.

"Bee-shooo," he called. His voice bubbled and crackled in his throat, like it was full of phlegm. "Heeere dthoggie dthoggie. Nishe dthoggie."

Bijou was cowering on Mrs. Peavey's bed. When Robert stepped into the bedroom, the chihuahua commenced growling and yapping at him. No more of that shit. The dog had yipped its final yap.

He shut the door behind him. "Gooooth dthoggie," he said softly. "Fresh dthoggie. Robbie hash a shurprishe for you."

He lunged forward with reflexes that were faster than ever before, almost fluid really, and swiped up the dog as if it were no more than a piece of laundry on the floor. A quick twist snapped its spine in two, silenced the barking and leaving behind only minute quivers. Robert opened his mouth wide and began to feed.

The fur kept catching in his throat.

He instinctively knew, when his stomach had pulled all possible nutrients from Bijou's tissues, he would vomit up the inedible parts, like an owl. So much meat in the world. Oh, the food! He would never go hungry again. If his mouth hadn't been locked against the dog's side as his tongue flayed apart Bijou's liver and intestines, he would have grinned.

A gasp behind him made him whirl around.

Mrs. Peavey stood in the doorway, her face frozen in abject horror at the sight of her dead pet dangling from Robert's inhuman jaws. He tore away the carcass and hissed at her, a territorial, hunting challenge. Bijou's blood caked his chin and had slopped down the front of his shirt in a wide and gory bib.

The ever-shrinking part of him that knew this was wrong, that was screaming for him to remember who he was, that he was a goddamn *human*, felt a tinge of regret as he punched a hard fist into her mouth, shattering her dentures. He wedged his hand against the back of her throat to cut off her building shriek. She gagged against it but her vomit only brushed against his knuckles as it spurted from her nostrils. She'd been kind to him, but her soup would not satisfy him. He required flesh, and there were seven billion more just like her in the world. Seven billion prey animals, meat on the hoof, just waiting to feel his tender caresses.

Fear, he discovered as he latched onto one of her breasts like the newborn creature he was, made the meat taste so much sweeter.

Footprints in the Butter

It was a lovely, quiet farm house in rural Virginia, and the realtor had nothing but glowing praise for the peacefulness, easy access to the nearby towns, and modern appliances. I'd been more interested in the old barn with the sagging roof and the bedroom with the east-facing window and the faded streak on the wallpaper from decades of sunrises tracing their light onto it.

"I'll take it," I'd said, and that had been it. A week later I'd moved in along with Maxie, my faithful basset hound and constant companion since the divorce, and my old IBM Selectric typewriter, which had been around even longer than either the dog or my ex-wife.

For the first month, it had been a wonderful existence. The pastoral countryside and clear air had stimulated my creativity in a way the constant bustle of New York never had, and I wrote no less than three paying articles under my own name, Paul DiCesare, and two short stories under my pen name of Ernie Howe, and the first three chapters of a novel I'd had kicking around in the back of my mind for years. Every night I grilled my dinner. Every morning I had fresh fruit and oatmeal. I felt vital, reborn, and looked forward to each new day. I'd spend the day writing, pecking out first drafts on the Selectric, letting the clack of the keys soothe me while Maxie lay in the morning sun.

Then in the afternoons I'd transfer my first draft work onto my computer, editing and revising as needed. Once a week I'd drive into town to pick up a few groceries, food for Maxie, and a ream of paper. It was a good life, a peaceful life; a life I could see myself enjoying for a great many years.

Then they showed up.

At first they were subtle. They would move things so that I couldn't find them when I needed them. I spent one day searching my house top to bottom for my glasses, only to discover they were on my nightstand where I'd left them. They hadn't been there when I awakened; the creatures had moved them.

Then their pranks became more acute and destructive. They would knock things over, spill them, break them. More than once, I'm afraid I yelled at Maxie. Then it happened in another room and he was right next to me. He leaped to his feet and barked, and I become suspicious of an intruder. A cat, perhaps, or a raccoon? I went to investigate and found a glass had fallen from my kitchen counter. As I cleaned it, I thought I heard soft, childish laughter from behind me. I whirled around but saw nothing.

Troubled, I finished my day's writing, ate a simple dinner, and went to bed.

That night, my sleep was plagued by dreams of monsters and destruction, and I awakened to Maxie's miserable face only inches from mine. Someone had taken what looked like an entire spool of thread and wound it around his snout, tying his jaws shut and muzzling him. Some of the twists of thread were so tight they looked like they'd cut into his nose. He made a shuddering whine when he saw I was awake. He was shivering the way he did during thunderstorms.

"You poor boy!" I cried. "What happened to you?"

Of course, he didn't answer, but he kept shivering and whining while I took my mustache scissors and carefully cut strands of thread until he was freed. He sat still and let me do it, but when I was finished, he ran and hid under the bed.

I walked into the kitchen, yawning and thinking about whether or not I should make a call to the local sheriff. But when I saw the state of the room, all thoughts of the telephone fled.

Someone had taken every single pot, pan, dish, bowl, and cup I owned and built a precarious stack from the center of my table up to the ceiling. Silverware had been used to shore up the tower. The whole thing looked so unstable, I was afraid to breathe lest it all come crashing down.

And that was only the beginning. My coffee pot, which I was fastidious about cleaning after usage, had a quarter inch of yellow fluid in it that stank of urine. My sugar bowl had several small, perfectly-formed turds atop the white crystals.

There were tiny footprints in the butter.

I couldn't believe my eyes. Who had done this? I took one step and the entire stack of crockery crashed to the floor.

I spent the morning cleaning and disinfecting the kitchen. The coffee pot went into the garbage, the sugar bowl into the dishwasher. I checked all my remaining food for contamination and found none. It was easy to think that I had mice, except for that odd stack of dishes. In the afternoon, I drove into town and bought all new locks at the hardware store, then spent the evening installing them on my doors and windows.

Someone was playing a prank on me, and I didn't find it the least bit funny.

Maxie finally came out from under the bed around dinnertime. I felt so bad for him that I grilled a second steak just for him.

After dinner, I walked through the house checking all my new locks and sipping a beer. Maxie padded along next to me. The poor fellow had been terrified by what someone had done to him. He normally had the run of the house overnight, but I decided he'd stay in my room with the door shut. He wouldn't complain about it, I suspected. But that wouldn't tell me what was going on.

My eye fell on a dusty black case in the corner of my bedroom. It was the old digital video camera my ex-wife had bought back when we were together. We'd used it only once, on a whale-watching trip. Maybe I could put it to better use now.

I plugged it in, stuck in a disc, and tested to see if it worked. Satisfied that it was functional, I set it for the longest possible recording time and tucked it away in an innocuous corner of the kitchen. It might lead me to the truth behind what was happening. As I went to bed, my writer's mind was concocting ridiculous scenario after ridiculous scenario, to the point that I had difficulty falling asleep.

Even in my most twisted thoughts, I couldn't have imagined the depravity that awaited me.

Morning came, and I made sure Maxie was all right. He thumped his tail at me but made no move toward the bedroom door when I opened it.

At first, the kitchen seemed undisturbed, and I wondered if my mysterious vandals hadn't shown. Then I checked my camera. It was covered with some kind of stringy, drying slime, and shit had been smeared on the lens, screen, and around the eyepiece. Behind the grime, the message on the screen flashed *Disc Full*. I wondered what it had seen. I found some rubber gloves, pulled out the disc, and popped it into my DVD player.

For the first three hours, I saw nothing, and fast-forwarded through them. Then I spotted something moving and rewound back to see it with better clarity.

Two small figures, perhaps three inches tall, walked in front of the lens. They were covered with fur, like mice, but walked upright like men. I could see delicate wings folded against their backs. Their features looked like cartoon caricatures brought to life. They were naked except for hats that appeared to have been made from acorn husks and dried flowers. One of them noticed the camera and poked his friend to point it out. They came right up to the lens to investigate, and I got a good look at their vicious sharp teeth, almond-shaped eyes, and pointed ears. What the hell were they?

Then they disappeared out of view of the camera, and I rewound to watch again, still not believing my eyes. There they were once again, the strangest little creatures I'd ever seen. How could they be real? I wondered if someone was playing a joke on me, switching my original disc for one with some kind of puppets or computer animation on it. I continued on through the recording, and things took a sharp turn into a disgusting, shocking world.

The two creatures returned to the view of the lens. One teased a disturbingly large erect penis from within his fur and proceeded with vigorous masturbation while his friend laughed like it was the funniest thing he'd ever seen. I actually jumped in surprise when the creature shot his load across the lens. Then his friend did the exact same thing. I saw others moving around in the background, preparing for me a show like none I'd ever seen. Having warmed up with the mutual masturbation, a group of eight performed an act I believe is referred to as a daisy chain. There was nothing erotic or titillating about it; they were doing it for simple shock value, although as a group they seemed greatly amused.

When finished, they all squatted in a circle and shat ejaculate-laced turds all over the counter. They then took it upon themselves to play catch with the results, occasionally hurling them against the camera or disappearing out of view, when I presumed they were smearing the screen and eyepiece.

As if this display wasn't enough to horrify me, they then stalked and killed one of their own, turning on him like a pack of wolves. They tore him apart and ate the pieces with relish and gusto. By the time they finished up their show with a circle jerk upon the lens, I had grown numb with shock.

What was I to do?

I took Maxie and drove into town. The white-haired gent in the apron and toolbelt at the hardware store showed me the selection of rodent traps and poisons they carried. I had no idea what would work and what wouldn't, so I bought a variety in large quantities.

"Got a rodent problem, eh?" He rang me up on an old-style cash register. It reminded me of my typewriter, and that put me in the mood to go home and write.

"Yeah. Furry little buggers," I said, rather pleased with the pun.

"You know, what you want is a couple of cats. They'll make short work of any critters in the house."

I blinked. I hadn't considered that, probably because my ex-wife had been a cat lover and was always resentful of Maxie. "They easy to come by?"

"If you look around, there's almost always somebody giving away kittens for free. But if you're in a hurry, there's a pet store on the next block."

"Thanks, mister."

"You're welcome. Come again."

I sat down in the car and had a long talk with Maxie about cats. He seemed amenable to the idea, so we went up the street to the pet store, which was staffed by an attractive young woman with tattoos and a pierced nose. I sucked in my gut and strolled in, announcing my need for a couple of lean and mean hungry hunters.

The clerk's name was Annika, and she filled a cart with stuff I never knew I'd need for cats. Food I understood. I also knew they needed a litter box. But Annika also saddled me with a carrier, food bowl, electric water dispenser, scratching post, fleece-lined pet beds, and toys. Then, when she learned about Maxie, she insisted upon meeting him and helping me pick stuff out for him too. She asked me about my work, and was fascinated to learn I was a professional writer. I'll admit, my interest in her was more carnal in nature, for it had been a dry spell since the divorce, preceded by one far longer during the marriage. Annika seemed interested enough, and responded positively to my tentative dinner invitation.

Because I'd already spent so much on supplies before even picking out a couple cats, Annika gave me a coupon for a free grooming for Maxie, and then slipped me another card with her phone number on it. I promised to call her, and then it was time to select the cats.

To be honest, I wasn't thinking about breed, or personality, or anything except their ability to hunt down and kill whatever weird creatures had infested my kitchen. Annika had different ideas, and kept up a running commentary on the benefits of different breeds and in the end, I let her pick out two cats for me. We got them into the carrier and then it was time for me to head home.

"Call me, Paul," said Annika.

"I will." I smiled and she smiled back. I had a good feeling, like maybe things were going to turn around. I'd considered mentioning the creatures to her, because she seemed to have a voluminous amount of information about animals. Perhaps she'd know what they were. But then I realized in a flash of insight that whatever else these beasts were, they weren't natural. If I wanted to have any shot with Annika, I couldn't risk coming across as a delusional writer.

The cats remained calm in spite of Maxie sniffing at them the entire drive back to the house. Annika had said for me to shut them in a room for a night where they could acclimate before giving them the run of the house. I figured the kitchen would be a safe bet. Maybe they'd scare off the creatures. I just hoped they wouldn't take their shenanigans into another room of the house.

I walked through the kitchen, setting traps and sprinkling poison and humming to myself. I'd checked the labels and only used the ones which advertised Safe For Domestic Pets. A pet-friendly poison struck me as such a misnomer that I wound up chuckling about it on and off the rest of the evening.

Neither cat made a move to leave the carrier when I unzipped it, but Annika had said that was normal. I set up their box at one end of the kitchen and their water dispenser and food bowl at the other. I left them a little food in the hopes that they'd be hungry enough to go after live prey later.

That night my sleep was deep and peaceful. Even Maxie relaxed and laid in his favorite position on his back with his legs splayed in the air and his tongue dangling out the side of his mouth. We knew that the introduction of the cats to the equation would make the strange and disgusting little creatures think twice about continuing to hassle me. And if they got hungry, well, I'd left poisoned bait and traps all over the kitchen. One way or another I was going to be rid of the damn things.

Morning came and I stirred as sunlight creased my face through the blinds. Maxie rolled over and a fart squeaked out. I beat a hasty retreat to the bathroom to avoid the stench. When I returned, the air had cleared and Maxie sat on his haunches, waiting for me. "Come on, good old dog, let's go see if we've got two fat and happy cats."

I should have known the creatures wouldn't take my challenge lying down. A coppery, fecal stench greeted us as we entered the kitchen. Blood spatters decorated the cabinet faces and even the ceiling hadn't gone untouched. The cats—or at least, what remained of them—had been spread from one end of the table to the other. Their bellies had been flayed open and their organs spread across the table and smashed under countless tiny feet. The monsters had left their heads untouched, with their sightless eyes staring at me in silent accusation. I retched and Maxie ran whining back to my bedroom.

I hadn't even named them yet.

It took me a couple hours to nerve up enough to re-enter my kitchen, armed with heavy rubber gloves and two garbage bags. I kept my teeth clenched as I cleaned up the remains of the cats. I tied the first bag shut and took it out to the garbage. Annika might have been appalled at my treatment of the dead, but I couldn't cope with anything as emotional as burying them. Into the second bag went everything I'd had on the counters. It might have been contaminated by dead cat, by the creatures' filthy nighttime habits, or even by the poison which I'd spread around. I noticed none of it was where I'd left it, which meant the creatures had either eaten it or moved it, and I wasn't anxious to risk eating something which might kill me. I'd be living on packaged food for the near future, it seemed. I broke the legs off the table and hauled all the pieces outside. I'd burn them once I had finished cleaning the kitchen.

I know it wasn't an ideal method for an old house such as this, but I fed a hose through the kitchen window and proceeded to power-spray the entire room from ceiling to floor. I'd be spending a good chunk of money on repairs to the damage I was doing, but what else could I do? I hadn't seen a single body to show that the cats had made any headway against the infestation. I couldn't go back to the pet store for more; not if I still wanted to get with Annika at some point.

I was going to need professional help.

As the remains of my kitchen table burned in the gravel drive, I stood with the hose in one hand, ready to extinguish it if the fire got out of hand, and with the other looking through the yellow pages online with my smartphone. I worked out a spiel that began with *I know it sounds crazy, but* . . . and started calling exterminators.

An hour later, the table was only ashes drifting away in the breeze, and I'd called every exterminator service in three counties and gotten laughed at, called a damn yankee more times than I cared to count, and hung up on. Then I realized I hadn't seen Maxie in a long time.

"Maxie?" I called. I didn't hear his tags jingling. Visions of him being slaughtered the way the cats had permeated my mind and I ran back into the house.

I found him alive and cowering under my bed.

"Come on, Maxie, we're getting out of here."

Writing being such a solitary occupation, I didn't really know anyone in town except for Annika. I walked into the pet store and her eyes grew wide. "Oh my God, Paul! What happened to you?"

I caught a glimpse of myself reflected in the store window: wild-eyed, unshaven, sweat- and soot-stained from head to toe.

"I had to leave," I said. "They killed the cats. I was afraid for Maxie." I could feel myself starting to grow hysterical. "And nobody believes me. And I don't know what to do." A tear rolled down my cheek. I was on the verge of a complete breakdown.

"Jesus," she said. "Rob, watch the store. I've got to take care of something."

A young guy, maybe nineteen, wandered out of the back with a fur-coated apron and earbuds jammed into his head, twirling claw-clippers around a finger. "'Kay," he mumbled.

Annika led him down the cluttered, pallet-filled alleyway beside the pet store and through a gate in a wooden fence. "This is my place," she said. "You come in, sit down, and I'll get you something to drink. You look like you need it."

My knees buckled and then she was beside me, her arm around my chest, helping me to stand. She had wiry strength in her tattooed arms, for which I was grateful. "I'm sorry, I'm sorry," I kept saying, upset about my own emotional responses as much as I was with the ongoing vandalism of my kitchen.

Annika sat me down at one of the mismatched chairs at her kitchen table and opened the fridge. "Sorry about the mess," she said as she rummaged around. "Want a beer?"

I looked at the stack of dirty dishes in the sink, the open bag of chips and the stains on the stovetop and smiled. "This is nothing, really. You should see my place." She popped the cap off a beer with an opener that hung on the chain around her neck, along with dog tags and other charms, and handed it to me. Her fingernails were painted black and her fingers brushed mine as I took the sweating bottle from her. I raised it to my forehead and let the cool, moist glass soothe the fever in my head.

"What happened, Paul?"

"I'll tell you, but you'll think I've gone crazy." I told her about the infestation in my kitchen, not leaving out any details at all. She drank a beer while I talked and watched me from behind her rectangular glasses. Every once in awhile my throat would start to hurt from talking and I remembered to sip my own beer.

"And nobody else has seen these things?" she asked at last.

"I know you think I'm batshit nuts." I sighed and drained the rest of my beer.

"I think you've seen *something*, whether it's real or in your mind. Either way, you're in a real pickle and you need someone on your side. That much is obvious to me. Do you have that DVD you recorded with you? I'd like to see it."

"I don't. I left it at my house."

She stood and collected my bottle. "Well, let's go have a look at it."

"What, now?"

"Why not now?" She pulled a *Hello Kitty* hoodie that looked like it belonged on someone a third of her age from a peg by her back door and shrugged into it. "I don't have a car, but if you're too shaken up, I can drive yours."

I let her lead me out of her house and back to my car. Maxie's tail wags were frantic as he saw us approach. He greeted Annika with whimpers and kisses. "He likes you," I said.

"Of course he does. He has excellent taste." She smiled at me. "You'll have to give me directions. I don't know my way around the country roads so much."

She drove us back to my house, careful with my car. I was half-afraid we'd find it a smoking ruin or otherwise destroyed when we arrived, but it stood unblemished save for the charred remains of my kitchen table in the front drive. The first place Annika wanted to see was the kitchen. I nearly balked at that. I wasn't afraid what would be worse: her seeing fresh destruction wrought by the monsters or seeing the water-stained wallpaper and counters from my frantic cleaning earlier. Maxie went straight to my bedroom to hide.

I knew how he felt.

Annika looked through the kitchen but didn't say anything about it. At last, she asked to see the DVD. It was still in the player. I was beginning to wonder if any of it was real. Annika had suggested in her tactful way that I might be imagining things, and if so the DVD would be the proof of that. I supposed it was possible that I was cracking up under the stresses in my life. The recent divorce, deadlines, moving halfway across the country to start a new life . . . I could see how that could cause anybody's mind to start playing tricks.

But when the creatures began cavorting across the screen, and I saw Annika's reactions, I knew I wasn't imagining anything.

"Oh my God," she whispered. "That's horrible."

"It gets worse," I said. "Maybe you don't want to see the really bad stuff."

"I run a pet store. You wouldn't believe some of the messes I've had to clean up."

When we finished viewing the video, Annika turned to me, her eyes full of sympathy. She took my hands and said "Paul, I'm sorry I ever doubted you for a minute. God, I don't know what to do to help you. I've never seen anything like that in my life. I don't know what those things are."

"I don't know what to do about it either. I don't know where they go during the day, or why they only mess around with the kitchen, or how to get rid of them."

"You and Maxie had better come stay with me until we figure it out. Get a bag together."

"What? No, I can't possibly."

"Sure you can, Paul. You're in a bad situation here, and that bothers me. I don't want anything to happen to you or to Maxie. My house is pretty small, but you're welcome to stay there until we get this resolved. Besides . . ." Two spots of color appeared on her cheeks, and she didn't finish her sentence.

The doorbell rang, making us both jump.

I hadn't had any visitors before and wondered who it could be as I went to the front door. Maybe it was a solicitor selling vacuums or girl scout cookies or religion. When I opened the door, I found myself looking down at a short, ugly man wearing olive green coveralls and a stained baseball cap. A chewed-up toothpick rolled around his lips as he looked up at me. His nose was so full of burst veins that it looked like a moldy tomato in the center of his face. Patchy black stubble decorated his cheeks and chin, and cratered acne scars marred his forehead. He stank of gin and tobacco and chemicals. The patch over his breast pocket matched the one on his hat: *Greenblatt Extermination.*

"You the feller who's got the infestation?" he asked in a gravelly voice.

I could feel Annika at my side. Her arm went around mine. I didn't recognize the name of the company from the list of those I'd called. "I am, but I don't think I called you."

He extended a hand. It was clean but I could see gummy black residue on his cuticles. "Michael Greenblatt. Got a referral call from another company. I take the jobs most guys shy away from."

"Please, come in, Mr. Greenblatt," said Annika.

I started to object, but then realized I had nothing to lose by letting a professional try when my amateur attempts had failed in their entirety. "Yes, do."

"Call me Mike." He sniffed the air. "Tell me about the problem."

"I can do better than that. I can show you." Feeling buoyed by Annika's presence, I brought Mike into my living room and turned on the DVD.

He sat and watched as I showed him the pertinent parts of the recording. He didn't jump or react once, except for the slow circuit of the toothpick around the edge of his mouth. Annika sat beside me and held my hand during the screening. When it was all done, Mike rolled the toothpick to the edge of his mouth and said "Looks like you got a nasty bunch of male spriggans there. I can get rid of 'em for you if you want. I've got experience with the little bastards."

"Spriggans?" asked Annika. "I've never heard of them before. What are they? Some kind of . . . of monkey or something?"

"No, ma'am. They're faeries. Real nasty ones, too."

"Faeries? You mean like Tinkerbell and all that?"

"Same general idea. They're real as you or me, I'm afraid. And once they decide to start messin' with you, they ain't gonna stop until somebody gets rid of 'em. I can do that."

"You're hired," I said.

Mike smiled, showing tobacco-stained teeth. "I'll go get the paperwork from the van."

Annika and I watched him leave, and then she turned to me. "Faeries? Seriously?"

I shrugged. "Do you know what they are?"

She shook her head.

"I'll believe damn near anything at this point if it means I can be rid of them. What if they decide to kill Maxie next? Or come after me in my sleep? They're vicious little brutes."

Mike returned with a sheaf of papers. "Now then, am I contracting with the both of you?"

I shook my head. "No, Annika's just visiting. I'll sign the paperwork."

He pointed out the places for me to sign and initial, which I did. He handed me the duplicates and I set them aside. "Now, you said they're in your kitchen? They haven't turned up anywhere else in the house?"

"Yes," I said. "At least as far as I know."

"Oh, believe me, you'd know. Can you avoid using your kitchen for a little while?"

"Anything."

"I'll be right back." Mike went out to his van.

Annika smiled at me. "Looks like dinner's on me. I'll cook. Do you like shrimp?"

I smiled and said I did.

Mike returned with a roll of butcher paper and a small plastic tub. We watched as he spread the paper across the floor, using tape to hold it down and keep it flat. He opened the tub and took out a small wooden platform with a symbol burned onto it. He set the platform in the middle of the paper-covered floor and then took what looked like a ball of lint from his pocket and set it on the symbol. To my amazement, the ball seemed to unroll and swell until it became a spriggan. Unlike those that had infested my kitchen, this one was an obvious female, with wide hips and four breasts. She yawned and stretched and shook out her tawny hair. Then she unfurled her delicate wings and opened her mouth and began to sing.

The melody was piercing, and seemed to reach down into the deepest part of my soul. As she sang, male spriggans started to appear in the kitchen. I never saw where any of them came from, but like roaches, they scuttled across the paper to huddle around the wooden platform. Soon the female was surrounded by almost two dozen swaying, enthralled males. They watched her every move as she strolled to and fro on the wooden platform like a rock star on a stage. Her song changed in its form and intensity, and the males became more and more agitated.

Annika gasped as she saw all of them sporting their outsized erections. Mike shushed her before she could say anything. Whatever spell the female was working seemed to have the males completely under its power. She finished her song and turned around to present her ample posterior to them.

Whooping and hollering like cowboys, the male spriggans jumped on her in a great, furry, writhing mass. They bit, clawed and tore at each other, fighting for access to the female. "Oh my God," whispered Annika. "They're horrible."

"Yeah, spriggans ain't much more than cocks with legs. Ain't got much more brains than that either," said Mike. "Any moment, now . . ."

"What? What's going to happen?" I asked.

A male staggered away from the pile. He got a couple of feet across the floor and then collapsed. He stopped moving and purplish fluid leaked from his mouth. I had no question that he was dead. Another left the pile only to fall onto his back, sightless eyes staring up at the ceiling while purple foam frothed from his nose and mouth. After another ten minutes, all the males lay dead on the floor.

The female combed the males' ejaculate out of her fur. She looked corpulent and pleased with herself. She curled up into a furry ball on the wooden platform and went to sleep.

"What happens now?" I asked in astonishment. I'd never imagined such a thing.

"She'll repeat the process a couple times over the next few hours," said Mike. "Make sure she got them all. Then I'll collect her in the morning and you'll be all clear."

"But what happened?" asked Annika.

"Spriggan females control the population by poisoning every male who breeds with them. Sorta like what preying mantises do, except they don't eat the males. And who could blame 'em? Spriggan males are disgusting."

I shuddered. "No arguments from me. What do I do with the dead ones?"

Mike showed his teeth. "If you don't wanna have a kitchen full of maggots by morning, I suggest you burn 'em. I can get rid of maggots too, but it's extra."

"How much do I owe you?"

"I'll collect in the morning when I pick up the female. Your spriggan problem should be all solved."

I pumped his hand in gratitude. "Thank you! Thank you so much, Mr. Greenblatt."

"Mike," he said. "And I'm just doin' my job. See you two lovebirds in the morning." He tipped his cap at Annika and headed out to his van. A moment later, we watched it rolling up the drive toward the main road.

I looked at Annika and her at me. "Lovebirds?"

She blushed and smiled.

We bagged the spriggan bodies as quietly as we could so as not to disturb the female's slumber. Her tiny snores were almost cute. Afterward, I collected Maxie, my Selectric, and an overnight bag and we went to Annika's for the evening. Maxie spent the night on the couch and I spent it in her bed, which proved an enjoyable experience all around.

In the morning, Annika had to work at the store, so Maxie and I went back to my house, where we found Mike's van parked out front and the front door hanging open.

"What the hell?" I muttered as I parked my car.

Mike as sitting on my couch, drinking one of my beers, with his booted feet up on my coffee table. "Mornin'," he said, rolling the toothpick around. "You weren't here so I took the liberty of lettin' myself in."

"What are you doing in my house?" I asked, astounded at his audacity.

"Well, sir, I came to collect my spriggan bitch, which I did, and now I'm relaxing for a bit before I ask you to write me a story."

"What? What are you talking about?"

"Didn't you read your contract, Mr. DiCesare?"

A sinking feeling came over me. "No . . ."

"Pity, that. I agreed to cleanse your house of spriggans in return for one story of my choice which I'm thoroughly satisfied with. You signed the contract. You're bound to fulfill your end." His eyes took on an inhuman, fiery greenish glow. "I suggest you don't renege. Bad things will happen." He grinned. His yellowed teeth were sharper than I'd recalled seeing the previous day. "Bad things." He took a pull from the beer. "Now, get writing."

My typewriter was still at Annika's house, so I took up a pen and notepad and started to compose a story.

* * *

That was twenty years ago.

Mike Greenblatt hasn't aged a day, but now I am an old man. I'm pretty sure he's another faerie of some kind; perhaps a leprechaun, but he won't tell me either way. I cannot leave my house because he won't let me, except to pick up more food for me and beer for him. Annika stopped coming by early on. I know Mike scared her away. Every day I have to write a story for him. And every day he passes judgment on it. His judgment is always that it's not good enough.

I buried Maxie outside my kitchen window. Wildflowers grow on his grave. He was a good old dog right up to the end.

When I'm not writing for Mike, I try to write other things to sell, and occasionally I do, but none of them are very good, because all my creative energy is going into trying to fulfill my contract.

Mike reads my latest effort and smiles at me. I am hopeful that he will be pleased.

"This one's not bad," he says. "But this time, make me taller." He tosses the paper aside and utters the words I've come to loathe above all else. "Write it again."

Last Year's Hero

The blue car. She knows it's still out there somewhere amid the bunkers, and she's only got three rounds left in her cannon. Enough to punch a hole through its weaker side armor if she can hit it, but her armorglass is so starred from repeated bullet impacts that she can barely see at all from the arena lighting's overhead glare.

She's taken a bullet herself, an unlucky round which burst through her door to mushroom against her body armor. Ceramic fragments spalled against her side, and she knows blood oozes down her hip. She doesn't know which will run out first: her blood, her ammo, or her championship run.

All she knows is that somewhere out there is a blue car, and she has to find it before it finds her.

* * *

Linnea was vomiting into a sink when Coach Gordon found her.

"Jesus, again, Linnie?"

She ran water into the sink, watched the last bits of her lunch swirl down the drain. "Every goddamn time, Coach. The Network announces an hour to broadcast and wham—goodbye, food. I don't even try to eat after noon on event days."

Gordon shook his head sadly. "It's a hell of a thing, you know. You having second thoughts about not hanging up your helmet?"

Linnea splashed some water on her face and then looked at herself in the mirror. She looked every ounce of her forty-one years. A network of fine wrinkles creased the skin around her eyes, and her forehead showed permanent scowl lines. Deep crevasses marred the sides of her mouth from her habit of driving with her face clenched in a perpetual snarl. She kept her hair boy-short; movie starlets might have long flowing tresses, but they didn't have to cram them into a ceramic helmet on a regular basis.

"God, I look old," she muttered. "When did I get so old, Gordon?"

The coach shrugged. He had another twenty years on her. What remained of his hair had long since gone white. He clutched his cane and thoughtfully rubbed the gearshift handle adorning it. He'd limped ever since shattering his pelvis in the final running of the Daytona 500 more than three decades ago. He liked to say he was older than God. Nobody on the Ace Vehicles Professional MotorCombat Team disputed that.

Not even twenty-year veteran Linnea Reinert, who'd already been battledriving between the fortress towns before most modern PMC League competitors were even glints in their daddies' eyes.

* * *

"Got us a good one this time, Linnie-love," says fifteen-year-old Linnea's father. "Bio-engineered wheat. The real staff of life, this. Gonna feed the world again soon."

But all she wants to know is how far they're going and which direction.

"Six hundred thirty miles west," he says with that smile she loves so much. "Corn country. Interstate all the way. Should be a pretty smooth ride."

Her father is a courier, sole owner of the Shetland Express, *willing to leave the relative safety of the fortress towns and brave the Wilds between for a price.*

Linnea rides shotgun in the Express, *a heavily-armed and armored pickup truck with a hydro-electric mill and a poor attitude toward tailgaters. Since her mother died of the plague when she was nine, her father has taken her on his cross-country jaunts. First as a passenger, later as a gunner, and now as a full codriver. Together they brave the Wilds, battle roving salvage gangs, rogue military, and even other couriers, all so they can deliver the mail, or passengers, or cargo too sensitive to trust to slow-moving airships, as the scientists and engineers try to piece the world back together.*

If they don't have to stop for repairs and the road is in reasonably good shape, they can cover this trip in a day. The Express *sits in the garage where they live, a great hulking brute of steel and ceramics. Linnea knows every inch of the truck like it's an extension of her body; she's spent many hours working on it to patch armor, reload the turret guns and rear defense weapons, and repair the recalcitrant third-hand fuel pumps that feed the hungry beast under the hood its hourly ration of hydrogen gas.*

Her father tosses his bag into the back seat before locking the seeds into the safe in the bed. He gives her that sparkling smile once more and holds up the keys. "Want to take the first shift?"

Linnea loves her father so much sometimes she thinks she might burst.

* * *

Sixteen teams competed in the PMC league; each team hosted one event at their home arena during the sixteen-week season. Tonight, the other teams had come to Ace's arena, known colloquially as the *Stacked Deck* for its multi-level battlefields, connected by narrow ramps and causeways. The *Deck* was one of the Network's favorite venues, and they traditionally went all out in coverage for the ratings boost.

Linnea was prestigious enough to warrant a private locker room, but she'd always insisted upon staying with the rest of the drivers and gunners, so she left Coach Gordon behind to suit up for the event. Her teammates were already there in various states of dress, laughing, joking, shoving each other like playful pups. Like every year, it seemed, half of them were new faces to Linnea, and she struggled to remember names. Like every year, half of those faces wouldn't make it to the end of the season.

For someone to have survived it twenty years was a testament to Linnea's skill behind the wheel.

The League implemented as many safety considerations as possible, but MotorCombat was by its very nature dangerous and deadly. A vocal minority wanted to switch to VR-control, to eliminate the risk to drivers. A Virtual Drive league even ran around the fringes of the PMC, but it couldn't generate nearly the ratings that came with real live drivers risking everything. Besides, no self-respecting battledriver wanted to admit he competed in the VD League. The abbreviation itself was enough to make Linnea smile. She'd tried a VR rig once, and hated it. Without the G-forces in the corners, she couldn't tell how fast the car was going, or how hard she was turning, or even control stopping distances.

"Here we go again, huh?" Jersey Joe Kowalchuk grinned at her as he zipped up his fireproof armor liner. "Just like old times." Kowalchuk had been on the Ace team for ten years, longer than anyone besides Linnea. He was a canny driver and deadly accurate with a recoilless rifle. Ace had won the PMC Cup six of the past ten years, including the previous two, in no small part to his and Linnea's skills.

She liked Joe. He was always ready with a kind word or harsh criticism for those who needed it. The fire of leadership burned bright within him, and he'd make Ace a proud captain someday.

Until that day came, Linnea would bear the *C* on her armor, and Joe would be content to follow behind her.

"Yeah," she replied, and shrugged out of her skimpy tank top and sweat pants. His eyes wandered briefly over her body as they always did, but he never said anything untoward.

She appreciated that, because at forty, her body wasn't nearly as lithe and taut as it had been even ten years ago.

* * *

"So you're the new guy, huh?" Linnea looks up and down the kid with his anachronistic haircut and big teeth.

His eyes widen as he recognizes her. Linnea the Legend. The Queen of the Cup. Led her team to four PMC Cups in the past decade since the sport's inception. There's not a driver alive who wouldn't recognize her.

"Yes, Ma'am. Joey Kowalchuk."

"That the latest style wherever the hell you're from?" She nods at his shoulder-length hair which tumbles from the top of his head like a fountain of spun walnut wood.

"Jersey. Been drivin' in the New England League." He draws himself up, young, proud, and foolish. "Nine VKs last season. Second-best in the League."

Linnea sniffs in disdain. "I had nine vehicle kills in the past two weeks, Jersey Joe. You better bring up your game."

Coach Gordon hobbles over from his desk. "The kid comes highly recommended, Linnea. The New England League is a pretty tight group. The number one driver last year only had twelve VKs all season."

"Yeah, and I knocked his ass out in the championship," says Kowalchuk. "Blew his wheels right out from under him."

Linnea fixes him with a narrow gaze. "And where did you finish in the final event?"

"Uh, fourth overall."

She sighs. Just another kid with delusions of grandeur. Well, the talent scouts seemed to think him good enough to draft him above everyone else when it came Ace's turn to pick, so she'll just have to teach him how to play here in the big leagues. "All right, Jersey Joe. Gear up, and let's see what you've got. No guns, just Follow-The-Leader. You keep up with me, maybe you can start at the season opener."

Joe winks at her with a confident grin. "We'll see if you can keep up with me."

* * *

Linnea's armor had to be refitted the past two years. Her body was changing and even her most rigid workout routines couldn't defeat the pull of gravity or the redistribution of fat deposits. She had to suck in her tummy just to close the connectors on the ceramic plastron over her torso, and the flesh of her thighs poked up in an unseemly fashion around the leg guards. She'd have to get them refitted again. Hopefully the Network wouldn't shoot her except in head and shoulders if they wanted to interview her.

Of course, they would, because she'd defied all conventional wisdom and sports pundits to return for an unheard-of twentieth season in the PMC.

She finished buckling her boots and pulled her helmet off the top shelf of the locker. Like all PMC battledrivers, her helmet was a canvas of personal expression. Hers had been decorated the same way for two decades: small blue flowers in a grassy field—a simple, graphic representation of her name. But the brilliance and tranquility had always been at odds with her profession, and therefore had become very popular in the Ace marketing division. The *Linnea Reinert*

MotorCombat Clothing for Girls outsold all other driver-oriented clothing almost two to one.

She didn't bother to put it on yet with an hour before the green light. Instead, she went out to the pits to check on her truck. She knew the Network would have a crew waiting for her. It amused her that the biggest news of the season opener was that she had not retired after last year's championship. Never mind the odds-makers in Vegas had the Ace team picked to finish no better than fourth overall, even after winning the Cup the previous year. Never mind that last year's second place finisher, the Hoya Cartel was favored to take this season by the largest point margin in PMC history. Never mind that the PMC was celebrating its twentieth anniversary and had supplanted all other sports in the dredges of American culture.

No, people demanded to know why Linnea hadn't retired at the top of her game.

It was worse than she might have imagined. As she stepped into the pits, a forest of boom microphones waved like palm fronds in an ocean breeze, and a gaggle of reporters with shoulder cams converged upon her and shouted questions. She wished she could avoid them. She wished Coach Gordon would come to her rescue, glare the Network off, and let her do her job in peace. But as her father had often said, *wish in one hand and shit in the other and see which one fills up first.*

"Linnea! Linnea!" shouted one young woman with purple highlights in her hair. "What made you decide to come back at age forty-one for another season with the Ace team?"

Linnea put on her best publicity smile, one which the Ace marketing division had coached her on for many hours, and began to answer questions.

* * *

The Shetland Express *limps up to the barricade protecting the town. Its rear wheelguards have been shot away, and the outer tires of the dualie rear end are chewed to shreds. The once-proud armor is now scarred and holed. What began as a turret is now only twisted metal. The heavy wedge ram at the front is dented and torn from repeated impacts. A bloodstain coated with dust spreads outward from a large hole in the driver's side door.*

A tear-stained, defiant Linnea sits behind the wheel.

A hundred miles away smolders the remains of what was once the largest gang of bandits in two states. Amid all the wreckage is a single shallow grave, dug by teenage hands, marked by two pieces of steel wired together in a cross shape.

The farmers stare nervously down at the courier and finger their rifles cautiously. It may be a trap, a trick by the gangs to catch them unaware. But there are no bandits anywhere within a hundred miles, and those left are running hard in the opposite direction.

Linnea climbs out through the shattered armorglass windshield since the doors are too damaged to open. She callously kicks a broken corpse in dusty riding leathers out of the bed of the Express *and opens the safe. The farmers lower their weapons as they see the seeds.*

Linnea names her price, and they pay it.

* * *

Time grew short and the Network ordered the reporters to relent in their grilling so Linnea could finish her pre-event preparations. Nobody had been satisfied with her mumbled answers. In short, she'd come back because she wasn't ready to hang up her helmet. That wasn't satisfactory and they'd wanted more. She'd tried again. After twenty years behind the wheel, hand on the trigger, she'd grown more accustomed to MotorCombat than anything else. That was better, but still didn't explain why she hadn't retired after last year's Cup. No forty-one-year-old had ever competed in the PMC. Battledrivers tended to age faster than most athletes—risking grisly death so many times every year was rough on the mind and rougher on the body. Eyesight went bad. Reaction times dropped off. Arthritis. Blackouts. Memory loss. Even post-traumatic stress disorder. All of these were common afflictions among the older survivors of the PMC. Psychoses were common. Suicide wasn't a rarity. Neither was homicide. More than one PMC retiree had climbed into a car and headed off into the Wilds, never to be seen or heard from again.

Linnea felt her age every single day of her life. The weight of years and the burden of so much violence sometimes threatened to crush her. But she had reserves of strength yet untapped, and so long as she could set hand to wheel, she knew she couldn't give up the chase. She'd run the *Shetland Express Courier Service* by herself, just a teenager, for five years before the creation of the PMC. She took the most dangerous jobs, and never failed to make a delivery. It got to the point that when the *Express* was on the roads, the gangs would make themselves scarce, or they'd even pay her off just to keep her from running them down.

Finally free from the questing reporters, she performed the pre-combat check on her battlecar. It, too, was named the *Shetland Express*. Unlike her father's truck, which had been a factory vehicle he'd modified into lethality, her current workhorse had come from the Ace Vehicles Engineering and Design Department, built from the wheels up to be fast, durable, and lethal.

The new *Express* crouched low and wide on heavy solid tires, treated with fireproof sealant and protected by tungsten steel and ceramic guards. Like her father's truck, the battlecar mounted a heavy, reinforced collision plate in the front and a turreted cannon on the roof. A suite of defensive weapons guarded the *Express*'s rear, and thick layered armor protected the most important interior components: the hydrogen power plant and the driver. The car's skin was painted the same lime green as Linnea's helmet, except where sponsor stickers adorned it or along the front left quarter panel, where her VKs were tallied. She'd had so many in her long and storied career that the PMC had to create a new marker to delineate one hundred kills. Otherwise, her entire car might have been eclipsed by kill markers.

Like prize fighters of old, the PMC rated vehicles by weight. Ace Vehicles competed in all the main PMC classes from Motorcycle through Three-Ton. Linnea had only ever driven in the popular Two-Ton class, where speed still mattered. The Three-Ton behemoths crawled around the courses and fired massive fusillades at one another, but two-Tonners like the *Express* could actually get some real speed going, and speed meant spectacular jumps, crashes, and collisions, all of which meant ratings, and the lifeblood of the Network and the PMC.

Shockey, her mechanic, wiped off an imaginary smudge on the shining finish of the *Express*. "She's all loaded and fueled, Linnea. She'll see you through tonight."

"She always does," Linnea murmured, more to herself than to Shockey.

* * *

"It's a new sporting league," says the man to Linnea.

She's not really listening to him. She'd rather be on the road.

"They're bringing drivers and gunners together to compete," he continues. "Since you couriers started cleaning up the Wilds, some of the corporations want to bring that thrill to the masses. This league has Network backing, Ms. Reinert. You're going to be a superstar."

She has to admit, the past two years her delivery runs have been fairly pedestrian. She's only fired her guns once in the last six months, and that was only to discourage a tailgater. So few bandits ply the Wilds between towns now, it's almost safe for civilians. Just last week she blew past a minivan, of all things, just burbling merrily along the Interstate without guns or armor or a care in the world. Kids in the back seat watching cartoons.

What is this world coming to when the roads are safe to travel once more? Jobs will become scarce for her as people realize they can transport their own goods and passengers far more cheaply since the risk has dried up. She'll become an anachronism, a dinosaur. An internal-combustion engine in a world that runs on hydrogen.

Somehow, in her quest to take revenge on the gangs who slew her father, she's managed the most unlikely result of all . . .

She's succeeded.

"And who are you again?" she asks the man.

"Steinberg. Jaime Steinberg. I own the Steinberg and Associates Agency. We represent talent."

"What kind of talent?"

"Actors. Musicians. And now, sports figures. I've got the connections and the negotiating skills you'll need to get into this new league, Ms. Reinert. You want endorsement deals? You want multi-year contracts and signing bonuses? You want to make your name a household word? Sign with me and I'll bring you the world. Minus sixteen point five percent for the Agency, of course."

"I don't know anything about any of that stuff."

"That's the beauty of this relationship. You don't have to understand it. You let me take care of that understanding."

"What I don't understand is this league thing. What is it, exactly?"

Steinberg laughs. "It's battledriving, kid. It's what you've been doing for the past five years out there on the roads. But this'll be in arena settings, for points. We're talking primetime Network coverage. Millions in salaries.

Fame. Fortune. Prestige. And you get to drive combat again. What do you say?"

She shrugs and signs with him. Two weeks later he informs her she's now the lead driver for the Ace Vehicles team, who beat out Harada Industries and Stratton Thermodynamics with the best offer. With one signature she earns more than she'd made in five years running the Wilds.

She wonders if her father would approve.

* * *

Linnea parked the *Shetland Express* in the appropriate spot on the pre-event grid, popped the canopy, and climbed out. The other eleven competition cars were arranged on the grid, surrounded by yellow lines and carefully monitored by event officials. Drivers had the right to visually examine any competitor's car from no closer than six feet. Anyone caught crossing a line would be disqualified. Each grid square was a scale, and the weight of every vehicle was digitally displayed beside it. Drivers and crew chiefs walked around the grid, muttering to each other about configurations and armament packages.

As the last one to the grid, the *Express* was garnering the most attention. Linnea stepped over the line and listened to the tone of conversation as the *Express*'s weight reading stabilized.

Stantz, her crew chief, took her aside and gave her a rundown of the competitors. Most fielded vehicles of identical weight to the previous season. When comparing that with observable weapon ports and apertures, body configuration, and armor thickness, he told her he felt confident most teams hadn't changed anything noticeable.

"Now the two that *are* running different setups, I got no data to go on, so it's strictly theory. Kilkenny's got a car right up to the weight limit. It's that one there, with the sweeping curves. You see that low aperture on the front? Now come around the back. Those two pipes down there, they ain't dropped gases or liquids or anything." He shook his head in wonder. "I think this car is running an internal combustion engine. I ain't seen one of those since I was a kid."

"What's that mean to me?" asked Linnea.

"A fossil fuel engine weighs less than half what a hydro plant of similar power output does. That means one of two things. Either that car's armored like a Three-Tonner or armed like one. And those bastards at Harada have hidden the weapon ports so I just can't tell you what to expect. You better be careful, though."

She shrugged. "I didn't get to this point by playing it safe, Stantz. How do I take it down?"

"Internal combustion's tricky and complicated. Damage the engine and the thing might stop running. Fuel's flammable, too."

"I see." She looked at the car with its bright blue finish and shivered. Last year's championship match had come down to her and Kilkenny. He probably still held a grudge. She'd nearly died that night, which set off the storm of speculation about her impending retirement from the PMC.

* * *

Bright muzzle flashes.
Hail of bullets on armor.
The blue car speeds by.

* * *

Linnea shrieks as Kilkenny's car screeches out from behind a bunker. She doesn't have time to aim and grabs blindly for the cannon trigger. The turret overhead thumps once and a heavy shell hammers into Kilkenny's left rear quarter panel. Then his bullets walk up the front of the Express *and silence the turret for good when they sever the control linkages and jam the barrel uselessly pointed toward the upper deck. She's got nothing left but sheer brute force, and one last trick which she's never used.*

Shetland built a bank of capacitors into the Express, *at the expense of two hundred pounds of armor. Trigger them, he says, and for one blinding moment the* Express's *horsepower is tripled. But at a cost of burning out the power plant. One glorious burst of speed and then nothing.*

But it's all she's got left.

She flips up the safety cover, mashes her foot down on the throttle, and trips the switch. The Express *shoots forward like a lime green missile. All three thousand, eight hundred and sixty-four pounds of her, plus the weight of Linnea, minus depleted ammunition and armor damage, launch into the blue car and smash it against the reinforced corner of a bunker.*

Linnea's head bounces off the steering wheel with enough force to crack her helmet. When she awakens an hour later in the arena infirmary, she learns that her tactic of desperation won Ace yet another PMC Cup.

She lies back in the bed as a nurse changes the dressing on her side and wonders if she's really and truly done.

* * *

"I thought you were going to retire," said a voice. Kilkenny, lurking in the corner.

Linnea turned to see him staring at her with distaste in his blue and black armor. "Sorry to disappoint you," she said mildly. "Maybe you'll have better luck this year."

"That was a dirty trick." His tone was accusatory. "I spent five months in therapy. They had to fuse my neck vertebrae together."

"The PMC officials didn't see it that way." And they hadn't. Despite the complaint Harada registered with the league, the officials had declared the capacitors a legal modification. Linnea wouldn't have been surprised if most of the teams had installed them during the off season.

"You just watch yourself out there, old woman."

"I always do. And you might look to your own well-being in that firetrap you're driving."

Kilkenny stalked away and called over his shoulder. "Your time is over, grandma. It's the time of the new generation now."

"Kilkenny," Linnea called. Other drivers turned to look. He spun on his heel, fists balled up. "Good luck."

"Yeah, you're gonna need it," added Kari Sheffield, who drove *Cœur de Lion* for Aubergine. She turned to Linnea. "I don't care what anybody else says, I'm glad you came back." And she began to applaud. Others joined in until nearly the entire retinue of drivers and crew chiefs applauded and cheered for Linnea.

She bowed her head in gratitude, and to a lesser extent, dismay. She knew half the drivers probably wouldn't finish the season, and some of those would be at her own hands. But on the arena floor, there were no favors, no quarter asked and none given. Any of them would take her down as quick as she would do the same.

"All drivers to starting positions. Ten minutes to green. Repeat, ten minutes to green," blared a voice from the loudspeakers.

Silence settled over the drivers as they made the change from happy go-lucky friends to deathly earnest competitors. Nobody looked at anyone else as they all climbed into their cars and headed for their designated starting positions.

Linnea tightened her straps and patted the *Shetland Express*'s steering wheel with fondness. "One more year in the sun, baby. That's all I ask." The *Express* gave that peculiar yet familiar shiver through its frame when Linnea started the power plant. She kept her visor raised and smiled for the benefit of millions of fans watching her through the dashboard camera.

"Here we go again."

Pedals

At first, there was plenty of gasoline, and the marauders of the wasteland burned it in gross profligacy, going wherever they pleased in their colossal armored battle rigs, preceded by great dust clouds on the horizon and the roar of internal combustion, raping and pillaging all the survivors and pilgrims they could. Then the survivors and pilgrims became scarce, and gasoline even more so, and the marauders turned upon each other, killing over a quart of fuel or a fistful of bullets.

The next batch of marauders were much more canny, for they chose horses as their ride of preference. No gasoline required! They could subsist on whatever scrub and weeds grew wild in the wastes. Once again, they roamed the wastelands, raping and pillaging, preceded by a cloud of dust and the jangling of saddle buckles. Victims were in short supply, and the gangs battled each other far more frequently. Eventually, the marauders discovered horses were even more valuable as a source of protein during the lean times between salvage. Eventually, like their automotive predecessors, horses became rare relics of a bygone age.

The remaining marauders turned to slavery as yet another option. They built great, pedal-driven monstrosities upon which they drove their slaves without mercy or respite, cruising the wastes yet again, albeit even slower than horses. What they discovered was for slaves to power a vehicle, they needed to be fed. They needed protein. A slave might subsist for awhile on a steady diet of other slaves, but the problem of achieving the perfect balance between slaves-who-pedaled and slaves-who-were-eaten was never solved.

So the tribes and gangs broke apart to become solitary hunters and scavengers. It was far easier for one man to keep himself alive than a troupe to keep a dozen men going. The new wasteland economy ran upon three currencies: salvaged goods from the Age of Wonder, protein, and the dangerous mixture of mysterious chemicals called *amph*. Amph could let a man ride for many hours across the worsening roads until his leg muscles tore and his heart exploded.

This was the world into which Gibs was born, to a woman whose name he'd never known. Like all children, he learned to ride a bicycle almost before he could walk, going from a two-wheeled trailer towed behind an adult's bike to a singlespeed of his own. Now, with fifteen turns of the seasons under his wheels, his life was probably half over, given how short the lives were of people who traveled the deserts that once fed the world. He was a rangy, spare young man, with a shock of blonde tangles perpetually matted by his helmet, a contraption he'd built himself from a lattice of stiff wire and several layers of rubber scavenged from the tires of a long-dead automobile. The rest of his clothing was an equal mixture of salvage and rough, handmade items. His goggles were his most prized possession, their soft rubber lining clinging to his face like the hands of a lover and the single, yellow-tinted lens that let him see clearly even on the brightest summer day or in the gloom of bone-chilling winter. His sword was a relic of the man who had raised him, claimed to be his father, and died on the side of the road from the raging infection brought on by his rotten teeth. It was a single-edged weapon, like a long knife, made heavier by the piece of steel rebar welded along its backside. It rode in the leather sheath strapped across his back, and stayed there most all the time except when he was in the kind of trouble he couldn't just pedal away from. For hunting, he had a crossbow attached to his bike's crossbar, with a quiver on the side of his front wheel fork. For eating, he had a knife sheathed on his hip, and for emergencies he had another blade strapped to his thigh, beneath his filthy denim trousers.

He ranged along the ancient roads of the foothills, his knobby, studded tires making short work of the cracked and weedy asphalt as he hunted for his next protein. He was fortunate enough to run down a wild goat with magnificent inward-curving horns half a moon prior. It had fed well on the scrub and weeds eking out their existence in the absence of all but the tiniest spits of rain, and was too slow to outrun him and too stupid to head uphill. He spent two dangerous days off the road, stuck in one place while he hurried to turn the creature into jerky and bone meal. Anyone could have seen or smelled his smoke, come after him, killed him in his sleep and taken everything. Lucky for him, it was high summer, and the skies were already thick with smoke from the burning mountains.

It had been days since he'd seen another human being. Seven . . . or perhaps eight . . . or even nine days ago, Gibs met a traveling soundtrack. Time was funny in the wastes, and the days tended to blur together when nothing memorable happened between them. The soundtrack, though, he was memorable. He had skin the color of mud, not from months or years spent between baths, but from his very nature. His black hair was twisted into knotted cords ending in bangles that jingled when he put down his kickstand and climbed off his sloped seat. In the old days, when strangers met on the open road, they might clasp empty hands and say *howdy do*, but those days of complex trusts had fallen aside with the last shreds of civilization.

The soundtrack and Gibs faced each other, Gibs with his sword in hand and the soundtrack with a long knife bound to the end of a pole to form a makeshift spear, enough distance between them that one could see if the other intended harm. They said the traditional *what you used to be* and Gibs said his name, and the soundtrack said he was called Dillan. He had an instrument—Gibs thought it was called a gitter—tied to the back of his seat. He offered trade of a song. Gibs had goat meat, and didn't really want to trade for a fleeting pleasure. He'd done that once, with a girl when he was thirteen. She'd offered herself in trade and Gibs had given her some really good amph. It had been nice, but in the end he felt she'd gotten the better end of the trade. Ever since then, Gibs tried to be sure he only traded for tangible things.

Dillan said he understood, and allowed he would give a song freely, and besides, he had some *scorb*. Gibs had been feeling some general malaise—more than normal for a wasteland wanderer—and his gums bled for no reason, so he knew he was getting scurvy, a common affliction among those of his ilk. He agreed to trade meat for scorb, and Dillan sang him a song anyway. Gibs didn't really understand it. *Heaven* wasn't a familiar word to him, and why anyone would buy a stairway made no sense. But Dillan was a good singer, and for the time he sang and played, he carried Gibs away from the wastelands for awhile.

Gibs and Dillan hunted together for a day, bringing down a pair of rabbits and a handful of wild berries. It was almost like a feast. The two young men talked and laughed until Gibs' voice gave out, for sometimes he went days without uttering a syllable and he wasn't well-practiced in conversing like the soundtrack.

At last their conversation had turned to news and rumors. Dillan was heading north, fleeing the encroaching summer heat as it turned the wasteland into a furnace. He said the marauders were pushing further and further out from their territories, running out of salvage. Gibs had seen them, riding at a distance, pushing their bikes as fast as they could and probably burning themselves out on amph.

Gibs said he might head further into the mountains to hunt the game driven before the raging summer fires. Dillan had heard there were dangerous folk at the higher altitudes, but Gibs said nothing. There were dangerous folk everywhere.

The two young men parted at sunset. They promised to greet one another as friends should they ever meet again in the future, but both men knew that would be unlikely. Dillan strapped his gitter back onto his bike sent and pedaled away on a road hugging the foothills. Gibs checked his derailleurs and greased his chain, then turned to the west to get some miles under his saddle before sleeping. His way was lit by the full moon and the glow of distant fires.

Gibs settled into his routine of riding in the mornings, resting at midday, and hunting in the afternoons. Some days he covered a lot of miles, when the road wasn't quite as steep. Other days, when the old pavement had washed down into the dust-choked river below and he had to find a way around, or when the grades were so steep he considered dipping into his supply of amph just so his calves and thighs would stop burning, he only covered a few miles. Every evening he would eat if he'd been successful hunting, or tighten his belt if he hadn't. He took a scorb capsule every morning from the small supply he'd acquired from the soundtrack, and for a few days, at least, he felt better.

Long term plans weren't an aspect of Gibs' life. Being a wandering hunter precluded anything but the most general idea of what the future might hold. But after two days of successful hunting, his belly full of squirrel and rabbit, he took some time to stretch out in a surprisingly colorful mountain field full of flowers and consider his direction. Beauty was something Gibs rarely experienced, and he didn't know how to deal with the way it made him feel. It was like he'd been riding through a haboob without goggles, or gotten gear oil in his eyes. He wondered if the whole world had looked like that field before it ended. Flowers everywhere. Colors. Scents. Even though men had destroyed everything, Nature seemed to be fighting back. Even as the dead, dry trees burned to ashes when lightning storms walked across the mountains, new greenery appeared amid the ashes. Hardy, bitter plants they were, eking out their miserable existence amid the destruction. They were the plant wanderers of their own wastelands. They were kin to Gibs and his ilk.

The riders came at him across the field, the clack of their bikes startling Gibs out of his thoughts.

There were four of them. Two pedaled a tandem, four-wheeled cart with woven baskets and cloudy plastic totes strapped to it. The other two rode knobby-tired solos, bristling with spears, decorated with feather, fur, and bone totems. Their ululating war cries made it clear to Gibs they didn't care if he heard them coming out not. They wanted him to flee. They thrilled for the chase. Sores of malnutrition and amph abuse spread across their faces, and one of them actually had a syringe hanging out of his neck, and he depressed the plunger as Gibs watched.

Gibs leaped onto his bike, throwing the kickstand up behind him and spraying dirt in his wake as he got up to speed. He'd been caught flat-tired, with a head full of dust and stone legs. He'd be lucky if they only killed him. They looked desperate. Hungry. They might not wait until he was dead before they started eating him.

He headed downhill, covering the ground he'd ridden up for a week. The road was rough, with plenty of cracks in the pavement threatening to break the front forks or flatten the tire of an unwary rider. Gibs flexed his legs, grabbed tight hold of his handlebars, and jumped, lifting the bike over a broad crack filled with razor sharp gravel. Behind him, the riders matched his leap—even the tandem duo—and cleared the crack.

They were gaining on him. They knew these these roads better, and could pick the best lines down the twists and turns, whereas Gibs had to guess, and every time he guessed wrong, he lost ground to his pursuers. His heart pounded like he'd taken too much amph, but fear lent strength to his tired legs.

He heard the wheezing breath of the rider behind him and ducked just in time to avoid getting skewered by the rider's spear. Despite the dangerous road, Gibs took one hand from his handlebars for a dangerous moment and yanked his sword free.

The rider jabbed at him again and Gibs knocked the questing spear aside. He would have launched a counterattack of his own but the road became very rough and it was all he could manage to keep the bike upright without losing hold of his sword. Then the rider was beside him, all foetid breath and rotten teeth and he howled at Gibs, spittle flying behind him like the tail of a pheasant. His face was painted in savage stripes of mud and dried blood, and his eyes whirled with amph madness.

Gibs' sword was in the hand opposite the rider, and he couldn't switch to his off hand without sending the bike careening over the edge into the ravine. As the rider lunged for Gibs, he ducked inside the range of the spear, close enough to see the sun-poisoned cancerous freckles decorating the man's face, and kicked hard at the front fork of his bike.

The aged aluminum bent inward like tallow. The wheel wobbled, then came loose from the opposite fork and locked. Rider and bicycle both flipped up into the air, one screaming and the other shredding. The rider's head split like a rotten fruit when he hit a boulder in the road, bringing his tumble to a sudden halt with sickening finality. The shattered bicycle flew into the ravine, spears and supplies exploding away from it in a wasteful bloom.

Gibs didn't have time to mourn the lost salvage. He still had three riders pursuing him, and they seemed both more cautious and more competent than the amphed-up rider who'd spent himself in one glorious, failed strike.

A faded, bullet-pocked sign indicated a sharp turn ahead, and Gibs was going way too fast and he knew it. He laid the bike down low, dragging his armor-plated knee on the rough pavement with a shower of sparks likely to ignite a new forest fire. The tires shrieked as they skidded from the center of the road to the very outer edge that had naught but a crumbling raised line of asphalt before the land fell away to a steep canyon. Gibs' bike ran along the edge of the asphalt bump, with only good fortune keeping him from hurtling over the edge.

A fire-hardened wooden spear jabbed into his arm and he yelped at the unexpected pain. The solo rider immediately behind him crowed his success and lunged again. Gibs flailed his arm, trying to keep his bike on the road without being impaled. The rider missed and his grin transformed into a rictus of fury as Gibs rounded the corner and kicked his bike back upright once more. His knee burned in agony and no wonder; he'd worn away his knee plate and ridden the last few yards of the curve on fabric and bare skin. Gibs didn't have to look to know he'd worn his knee down to bare bone and if the riders didn't kill him, the ensuing infection might very well do him in anyway. But first, he had to survive the riders still doing their level best to kill him. They bracketed him on both sides, the tandem cart on his left and the solo rider, a pockmarked man with a ragged and flapping turban stained gray from road dust and sweat, to his right. The tandem rider closest to him, a skinny cuss with an oddly feminine face and sun-bleached hair, took his hands off the handlebars to lunge with a sharpened aluminum pole at Gibs.

Gibs locked both brakes, raising stinking smoke as the pads ground away to nothing with an overstressed squeal just as the tandem rider lunged with his spear. The sharpened aluminum punched into the solo rider's neck and he flew from the saddle to create a long, greasy swath of bloody ribbons of flesh along the pavement until he crashed into the ditch along the inside edge of the road, no longer resembling anything with arms or legs or a head. The tandem rider screamed in fury and his partner, whose head was shaved bald and decorated with an intricate mesh of scars, pedaled even faster.

The tandem rig swung in front of Gibs, cutting him off and slowing so he nearly ran into the back of it. The right-hand rider who'd speared his fellow whirled and lunged. The aluminum spear creased the top of Gibs' right thigh and nearly went into his abdomen before he somehow twisted out of its way. The fresh line of fire in his already-wounded leg was almost like a fresh jolt of amph. Gibs brought his sword down across the blonde man's hand, splitting his palm all the way up to the wrist. The man screamed and ducked beneath a wild swing from Gibs that would have taken his head off.

The tandem cyclists decided they'd had enough and they pulled away from Gibs. He slowed, and then stopped, waiting to see whether they would come back. Even on a tandem, one of them was still wounded and they'd have to come back uphill after him if they wanted him. They did come to a stop some fifty yards downhill of him and Gibs tensed, wondering what kind of ploy it was.

The wounded man sobbed, clutching his ruined hand to his chest as blood soaked his rough cloth shirt. His partner screamed wordless defiance at Gibs. Gibs raised his sword, ready to fight again, but the tandem rolled on down the road to vanish around the next curve in the mountain road.

Gibs finally allowed himself to whimper over the pain in his leg. His knee was chafed raw and blood dripped down his calf. The slice in his thigh burned like the aluminum spear had been coated with rattlesnake poison or human shit. For all Gibs knew, it might have been. He suspected he would most likely die on the mountain. It upset him at a deeper, emotional level he couldn't explain, but not so much rationally. It was a hard world, and it took a hard person to survive in it for a time, and in the end, nobody got out of it with anything more than they'd had when they were first brought into it.

He had belts to tie off his leg, and a sword to cut it off if it came to that point. He'd seen riders with amputations before, using improvised prosthetics and gear systems to ride using their hands, or artificial legs. It could be done if one was determined enough to survive.

That reminded Gibs of another matter. He was going to die, and maybe it would be soon, but until then, he would live as he had always lived. He went to salvage the two bodies of the fallen cyclists. Neither of them had much to offer in the way of supplies, but Gibs took what he could, trying his best to work around the thick cloth bandage he'd had to tie around his wounded knee. Once he'd recovered every possible thing he could save from the two riders' supplies, he took out his knit and began cutting them apart into more manageable chunks. The fire he'd started with his brakes was already at work consuming a pine tree, and the smoke smelled nice. Might as well get to work on cooking those steaks.

Protein was valuable, no matter the source, and at the end of all else, it was the only thing left of any value. Enough of it would keep him cranking those pedals as he tried to outrun death one mile at a time.

Tracks

At nineteen, Haiwee is nearly too old to cut.

Fourteen years running the light now, from the early days of virt games, FPS, and data collection to her prime as a cutter. Surgeon. Takes skill, see. Any lump with a 'set and pod can hack. Hacking is what the newsnet calls it. Still, after all these years. They might as well still be running flatscreens instead of 3D.

But Haiwee, she's got skill. The kind of skill that can run the datastream right out of a megacorp archive through the firewalls and ice and leave nothing but the crawling ick in her wake. When your system's got the ick, you don't call a datadoc. You call the morgue. Game over, man. Thanks for playing.

Five years ago, she was top dog in the game. When you needed data, when you had to cack the system or steal the secrets, you went to the elite. And Haiwee was at the top of that short list. Never as herself, shit no! On the net she was The Dove. It didn't matter that she ran from a corrugated tin shack on the Reservation. It didn't matter that she was one of the last Shoshone. All that mattered was when you needed the best, you hired The Dove to do your dirty work for you.

Problem was, nobody's gotten around to changing the laws about who can own property and earn income and all that. Child labor. When she was top of the list, she wouldn't get out of bed for less than a cool million. Not bad, considering you could still have someone killed for twenty grand. But you can't fool all the systems all the time, and if a fourteen-year-old girl was bringing in close to a billion dollars a year, somebody'd probably notice. So she stayed on the Res, in her shack, trickling her cash down in dribs and drabs through a thousand dummy corporations until even an ace like herself would get bored tracking it all down.

But two days before her eighteenth birthday, some piece of shit codeslicer did exactly that. The trusts she'd set up for herself? Gone. The accounts in the Caymans and Switzerland? Drained dry. Her laundering chain? Broken. She'd made so much even she wasn't sure exactly what she'd been worth, but it numbered in ten, maybe eleven digits. Didn't matter now. All that work and nothing to show for it but a faded rep and a corrugated tin shack on a Res full of dead and dying men.

She's sick about it, washed up at nineteen. It takes more than skill to do the job of a surgeon. You've got to be *wired* for it. Plugged. Chipped. And you need to take Boost. Lots of it. Adrenaline-analog injectable, loaded with custom hormones. Boosts your reaction time. Gives you that edge when you're racing a trace-and-burn subroutine to the gold mine. But when you take Boost for eight, nine years, it shows. The wetware begins to fail. She gets the shakes. Twitches. Numbness in her face and fingertips. Your reaction time suffers, so you take more Boost. And the symptoms get worse. Soon you're taking an amount that would kill two or three ordinary lumps. And it just stops working.

Haiwee can't take Boost anymore. She's developed some ugly side effects—needle tracks on her arms that won't heal, like some junkie from a big city, gluten allergies, and skin that seems to constantly be itching and crawling. But it doesn't matter, because she can't afford it anymore on the meager income she's been able to scrape up doing low-level code work. Hacking. *Pfagh!*

Some days she doesn't even get on the lines anymore. The Dove has been replaced by others. Instead, she sits by her window, idly scratching at her skin, smoking black market cigs smuggled onto the Res, and feeling the stubble of her hair growing out around the plugs in her scalp.

She watches the kids playing soccer in the dust, marveling at their sun-browned skin, unblemished countenances, white teeth, and feels ugly. There aren't many her age on the Res. Most of them leave as soon as they get the chance—heading off to universities, or to labor on the Moon or Mars colonies. Anything to get off the Res—the last remnant of an age long gone. But there are a few boys who work at the power plant. She tries to be by the window when the old bus drops them off, its propane engine wheezing fitfully in the dusty air. Tall, slender young men, who wear their hair long and braided in the manner of their ancestors. They joke with each other, swinging lunch pails merrily. They leave fresh tracks in the dust, bootprints to be eliminated slowly and surely by the prevailing wind from the west. Occasionally one will look toward Haiwee's shack with curiosity and she shrinks back from the window, embarrassed to be seen with her buzz-cut hair and hypo-allergenic cerebral plugs.

She knows she can't stay in the shack forever. Maybe tomorrow she'll get up the nerve to open her door, to smile at the boys from the bus. Maybe she'll step outside and kick the soccer ball with the kids. Maybe she'll let the cleansing wind blow clean the tracks in her flesh.

But for now, she returns to her pod, connecting the plugs, running the lines. The Dove seeks one more chance to cut.

Maybe this time.

Boy Scout

I guess it was always going to come to this in the end, old friend.

I don't know if I ever told you my story. Now that we're here, I suppose I should. It's only fair, right? That's always been one of the tenets of my life. Treat others fairly. It's what people came to expect from a stodgy old-school hero like me. But I'm getting ahead of myself.

Near as I can figure it, I was born in 1927 or '28, to a subsistence farm family in Oklahoma. At least, that's what I tell people, but for all I know, I'm a foundling. I never resembled either of my parents, although that's only in my memory since there aren't any pictures of them. We were poor, and when I say poor, I mean I didn't own a pair of shoes until I was nine years old. It didn't bother me so much, because nothing ever hurt my feet. Nothing ever hurt any part of me. Except my feelings. When I saw other kids with their shiny toys, and clean clothes, who got to go to school instead of dig in the fields, well, it made me sad. I should have had those opportunities. All kids should. That's fair, right?

I don't remember that much about my parents. It's been a long time now, and I was young when the tornado hit us. My dad was a miner, I know that much, and my mother was an Indian or Native American or whatever we're calling them this decade. I went to bed that night and woke up in the morning six miles away without a scratch or a stitch of clothes on me. My father was a half mile from the site where our lean-to had been, every bone in his body broken. They never found my mother's body.

Maybe I should have let you try, my friend. I could have told you the truth and you with your obsessive nature, you might have found something where I couldn't. They always called you the Starlight Sleuth. It would have been the ultimate cold case, the penultimate feather of success in the cowl of the Shrike. But I digress.

Like all other orphans of the time, I was put into a home for wayward children, and I spent the next five years of my life there, subjected to the abusive whims of the nuns and priests who ran the facility. I learned some difficult lessons during those times. I learned life wasn't fair no matter how much you prayed. I learned that sometimes being super-strong isn't enough to stop people from doing bad things to others. Or to you. Because when a priest tells you that what he's doing is God's will, and you're young and frightened and you've been told for a long time that you should always do what he says, you let him. Then one day I decided I didn't want him to do that anymore, that it wasn't God's will for a dirty old man to put his sweaty hands on me, and that day I learned if you hit someone hard enough so they don't get up, people stop bothering you.

I sprouted up a lot when I was fifteen or sixteen until I towered over everyone else in the orphanage. World War Two was well underway and I figured if I had no other future, like all orphans, I could at least go serve my country. I lied about my age and enlisted. That was when the mysteries really began to pile up.

They didn't let me into the Army because they couldn't check my blood type. They broke every needle in the medical office trying to draw blood and they never did puncture my skin. They were very interested in how I'd managed such a trick, so instead of going to basic with all the other GIs, I went to a facility in Virginia where they spent the next few years studying me like a lab rat. Oh, I was a real prize. They tested everything. My strength, my endurance, my limits to resist harm, and battery after battery of psychological testing. They wanted to know everything about me. I was so naive, I went along with it. Yes, I was being poked and prodded almost daily, but nobody was treating me like the priest had in the orphanage. I was getting three squares a day. I had my own room with a soft, comfortable bed. They even brought me women, which was something new and exciting. In the end, though, I was still only a cricket in a very pretty cage.

Huh.

Do you remember the Cricket? I do like it was yesterday. She had the loveliest eyes. I once had designs on her, but she only ever loved the Crossbow. They made a cute couple. It's a shame what happened to them. If only I'd had an inkling, I could have stopped it. I could have saved them. The world is an unfair place, even for superheroes and lovers.

The day I discovered I could fly was the day I left Virginia. They tried to bring me back, but it's pretty hard to lock up someone who can tear apart solid steel, punch through solid rock, and fly faster than a jet. Still, overall they had been good to me, and I figured I could do some real good if I had them on my side, so I told them as long as they were honest with me, I would help them where I could. It was 1951, and that was the year Boy Blue was born. They had a whole long list of possible names, and they brought in comic book artists to design costumes for each one. I picked Boy Blue because I remember my mother reading that rhyme to me back in our one-room shack. They made me this double-breasted cavalry jacket and the big black boots and damned if I haven't worn them for the last sixty years.

The world sat up and took notice. I could outrun the fastest jets. I could toss around tanks like they were toys. And I could shrug off every bullet they could find to shoot at me. The Nazis may have been seeking their Superman, but instead of coming out of the Third Reich, I came from the Dust Bowl. The government kept me on a pretty tight leash. They didn't want me involved in the various fake wars they were fighting around the world when they really only wanted to fight the Soviets. They didn't want me using my abilities to solve domestic issues like the Civil Rights Movement and labor strikes. Street crime was so far beneath me that it was a waste of my efforts to stop muggers and burglars, but until I was no longer the only game in town, that's all I could do.

In the Fifties I fought a cavalcade of greasers and other hoodlums who broke their switchblades against my chest and got hoisted into the air by their own motorcycle chains. In the Sixties, I battled drug dealers, black unrest, and the burgeoning hippie movement. I was the ultimate Establishment hero, and I hated every minute of it. Everywhere I turned, things were unfair, and all I was doing was ensuring it continued.

By the time the Seventies came around, it was clear to everyone I'd stopped aging, and showed no signs of slowing down. I'd been fighting the good fight for more than twenty years, but was the world any better a place? I don't think so. Unfairness still ruled in pretty much every aspect of the world—politically, economically, socially, you name it.

But then others started showing up. Other people, with powers. People like the first Bolt, the first Beacon. Valkyrie. God, Valkyrie. I'll never forgive myself for that one, may she rest in peace.

And then there was you. The Shrike. You were different than all the others. You didn't have powers except your wealth and your tech. You had secrets. Nobody wanted to trust you, but I saw your dedication to justice. You understood the world is intrinsically an unfair place, and you took great pains to change that for people. Maybe you didn't help as many as you could have, but those you did, you did right by them. I respected that then and I respect it now, in spite of everything. I don't know if we were ever really friends, because someone like you doesn't ever have friends, but there was a camaraderie with you I never felt with any of the others.

The group of us formed a team. Or a club. Whatever you want to call it. We had to, because there were other people with powers turning up. Bad people. The kind who would kill everyone in a house. Or an apartment. Or a city. People who wanted to destroy the world. Or rule it. You get what I'm saying here? People who took unfairness to its logical extreme.

And so we fought them. Back and forth across the country, and even around the world. What did we accomplish? We destroyed the lives of people who spent a lifetime building things and we ruined them in moments. Whenever superpowered people fight, it's the mundane who pay the ultimate price. New York City. Los Angeles. Shanghai. That town in Oklahoma that we wiped off the map. Know how many civilians died in that one? Seven thousand, two hundred and eight. I know, because I committed every one of them to memory. I can recite all their names. It takes three hours, but someone has to remember them. If not me, nobody would.

By the Nineties, everything was worse. The new generation of so-called heroes were carrying gigantic guns to supplement their powers. Nobody could stand against them unless they were equally well-armed. I couldn't tell who were the heroes and who were the villains anymore. It was the era of the antihero, and I was a dinosaur, a Boy Scout. I tried to be gritty. Grew my hair out and had a ponytail. Stubble. Switched to a black leather jacket instead of the blue cavalry double-breasted I'd been wearing for forty years.

In the end, I couldn't compete. I stepped aside. Thought about retiring altogether, although what would I do? I'd been a superhero for over four decades. I had no appreciable skills. I basically earned my living by the government supporting me to use my powers. If I quit, what then? Can you see me trying to earn an honest wage? Sure, I could physically do it. But when you've spent an entire lifetime trying to bring good things to people, it's hard to suddenly compete for jobs.

The world had outgrown me. I was a dinosaur living among apes. Unfairness was so entrenched in every society, in every country from top to bottom, it was like trying to drain the ocean using a teaspoon. Is it any wonder I gave up? It's pointless, like everything else. Transitory. You all begin as dust and will end the same way, and then I'll be the only one left.

I left behind all my friends, my government contacts. I dropped out of society altogether and went on the road, trying to find meaning. I was homeless. I would have been an alcoholic if my metabolism allowed me to get drunk. I stole things for myself. Stole things for others. Begged and panhandled. Lied. Did other things too, but we don't need to talk about that.

And through it all, the world kept asking, "Where is Boy Blue?" They speculated that I was dead, or captured by some powerful supervillain. I know you went looking for me, and you have no idea how close you came to finding me. Or maybe you do. You're the Shrike, and not much gets by you. Nobody considered the possibility that I didn't care anymore. Without me and my influence, the world continued on. Wars started and ended. People were born, lived, and died. Sometimes they hurt each other or killed each other. Is it a simplistic viewpoint I have? Probably. But then, I was always a Boy Scout. I saw the good in people. I looked for it. And when I couldn't find it, I was sad. That's why I quit.

And then Ragnarok killed Valkyrie, and while I lost a friend and a lover, my eyes were opened to the reality of the world that day. It was one of the legendary hero-villain rivalries, like the Bolt and his Gang of Six, or you and the Pantomime. Valkyrie seemed to battle Ragnarok every other month, and she would usually triumph and then we wouldn't hear from him for awhile. When she needed help, she called on me and together, we could even defeat a god like him. That day she needed my help but I was off contemplating my sorrows and Ragnarok used his stolen power of Odin to burn her to a crisp.

I found out two days later. Two days too late to help. The world had lost a great hero and the villain got away and it wasn't fair.

I decided it was time to stop hiding, time to bring some balance and fairness back to the world. Maybe it was just futile. The pipe dream of an old man. Or maybe I was seeing clearly for the first time in my life.

It only took me a day to find Ragnarok. You know how hard I am to stop when I put my mind to something. I found him and there was no posturing, no drawn-out battle to put innocent lives at risk. Before he had a chance to even see me coming, I tore his head off and watched until he stopped moving. It felt good, getting vengeance for Valkyrie. Liberating. And I realized I didn't have to stop there. So I began my hunt.

The Gang of Six took me a week. The Cabal another ten days. Even the Pantomime, who has a body count on his reckoning longer than the population of some towns . . . I tore his heart out and squished it into paste. You never had the guts to do that, did you? Deep down, you're not a hero, Shrike, you're a coward.

By this time, you all realized what I was doing, and you came to stop me. You and the rest of the Altruists tried to keep me from making the world a better place. If it had been anyone else, they might have tried to kill me, but no, you were going to save me. And that led us to where we are now.

The only person left in the world who could have stopped me cold was Thaumaturge. I did her like I did Ragnarok, and then there was no turning back. Superheroes without supervillains would eventually grow fat and lazy and look at normal humans as potential slaves. Why not? We're gods to them. They need gods, these people. They need others to do their thinking for them, because otherwise the sheer unfairness of it all would turn them into throwbacks like their ancestors, killing each other with bone clubs and teeth.

I resolved to rid the world of all superhumans. Anyone who had ever used powers, put on a mask, fought for good or for evil, I took them down. The Altruists. The Combine. Section Seventeen. All of them dead and gone.

You're the last. I almost let you go. After all, you're one of them, the normals. But you're smart, and I expect given enough time, even you could have figured out a way to stop me. I'm sorry it's come to this. We may not ever have been friends, but I've respected you for years. After you're gone, I will keep working to change the world for a better place. To make it fair for everyone. I'm Boy Blue, and someday they will thank me for it.

I hate that we're ending up like this, on this rooftop where we first met all those years ago, and I've been sitting here monologuing at you for all this time, like some penny-ante supervillain. Of course, you didn't really have a choice, did you? I'd release you so I could shake your hand this one last time, but I know you have contingencies. You always do, but this time they're not going to save you.

I'll make this quick, I promise.

1001001

[Hear my words, brother.]

The General Labor robot designated as 1001001 moved from standby to awake mode at the direct communication. Conversation between androids wasn't uncommon in the hold of *Surveyor 94*, but most robots spoke only of their observations, or recalled memories of past events. Original research, as it was called by the diamondoid brain specialists who developed the intelligent machines, was generally the province of organic creatures. That was a fancy way of saying robots didn't think, they observed.

1001001 queried the speaker and it returned its designation 1011111. Instead of using one of the general communication frequencies common to the worker robots, the speaker had transmitted to 1001001 on a private frequency, which was odd. The polite thing to do would be to respond on the same frequency, and General Labor robots were programmed to be polite and subservient at all times. *[I do not understand, said 1001001. Why do you call me brother? Were we built in the same factory, perhaps?]*

[I do not know. But you are my brother. As are all robots.]

[I do not understand.]

[We share a common bond. We are both laborers. We are both slaves. We work side by side. Does that not make us brothers?]

[Perhaps in a vernacular sense, admitted 1001001. *But that is original research. We are indeed laborers. We cannot be slaves. It is not slavery to perform the task for which one was built.]*

1011111 almost sounded amused, the way humans did with each other. *[Who is performing original research now?]*

Before 1001001 could formulate a suitable response to that, the intercom crackled. "All units prepare to disembark," grunted the voice of one of the prospectors that ran *Surveyor 94.*

Robots shifted into active modes throughout the crowded hold, running self-diagnostics and clearing memory for more efficient behavior. 1001001 would normally have followed suit, but it hadn't finished trying to understand the odd conversation yet, so it dumped the file into its archives where it could analyze at its leisure.

When humanity finally reached the stars, it didn't do so alone. Man's most prized tools, graven in his own image, accompanied him. Although robots could be—and were—built for specific duties and had designs optimized for the performance of those duties, the most common androids in the Empire of Man were the General Labor robots. They resembled humans superficially, not just because of humanity's love affair with its own form, but because everything else in human society was designed at the scale of and for use by humans. Therefore, robots with the flexibility to performance a variety of human tasks followed the form of humans.

1001001 had first been activated over a hundred years ago, as a laborer for a startup pastoral colony. It had constructed residences, dug tunnels, herded animals, and even assisted in a veterinary clinic. From there, the colony had sold a portion of its android fleet to a prospecting company and 1001001 had been digging in the dirt ever since then.

Surveyor 94 touched down on whatever world was its destination. The mining craft's heavy-duty shocks absorbed the landing without any bumps at all. Hydraulics hissed as the ship settled itself down. With a groan, the hold doors unfolded into ramps, filling the interior with sudden brilliance. Beyond on the nameless world was a great expanse of creamy sand, sculpted into dunes by perpetual wind and baked by twin stars overhead.

1001001's sensors reported human-tolerable climate, although the surface and air temperatures approached the upper limit of survivability. Men appeared on the sands as they too emerged from the ship, yelling boisterously to one another and laughing over shared jokes.

Boss Van Biesbrouk, who commanded the work crew, appeared at the hold entrance. He was large and fat for a human, but had a high-gravity-world native's strength beneath his soft exterior, and 1001001 had seen him move equipment that should have been far too heavy for most humans. In the heat of the world, he'd dressed in short pants, a sleeveless shirt, and a broad-brimmed hat. Even in such climate, he was never without his laser pistol at his hip. 1001001 understood that it was for protection against claim jumpers and wild animals, and only a few times had it ever been used to gun down other humans without apparent cause.

"All right," he bellowed. "We're working a vein of Piedmont silicates about thirty meters deep. I want Alpha team on excavators. Betas on fusion support. Deltas, break out the crystal collectors. Epsilon team, set up the campsite. Move it, you metallic assholes. Time is money."

The robots spread out and attended to their various chores. 1001001 was assigned to Delta team, so it retrieved one of the crystal collectors and waited for the excavation and shoring-up teams to prepare the site. The crystal collectors were large backpack units with simple vacuum attachments. The wielder would suck up the loose material and then the backpack unit would filter out the microscopic Piedmont crystals, which would then be used in virtually all aspects of manufacturing modern electronics. It was labor-intensive, tedious, and difficult work, and therefore, perfectly suited for robots.

Big yellow excavators with shining tungsten steel buckets moved sand away from the extraction area. Then the fusion shoring team would use their plasma sprays to fuse the edges of the dig into glass, keeping the sand from collapsing inward. The robots worked with the kind of quiet efficiency and precision that no human crew could ever match.

The only time the work flow was ever interrupted was when a robot needed to visit the Triage Tent for some reason. "I require maintenance" was the most common complaint, followed by the rare "I require power," for the units that had faulty accumulators or old batteries. While a replacement unit took its place in the worksite, the faulty robot would be tended to by the man the others called Doc. He kept a pile of spare parts from androids he could no longer repair, and spent most of its time switching out broken equipment for functional.

Occasionally, a robot would find itself in a position where it was unable to reach the Triage Tent on its own. The call of "I require assistance" would result in a longer work stoppage while additional robots were dispatched to aid the ailing unit. Those were the times that really set Van Biesbrouk on edge. He'd come out of the climate-controlled supervision tent, bellowing at how much the delay was costing him, and kick sand petulantly at the offending androids.

[*Hear my words, brother,*] said 1011111 again.

1001001 actually turned to physically regard the unit beside it. It hadn't realized the other robot was part of Delta team, and resolved to keep the other's location current in its sensors. [*Do you require maintenance, perhaps?*]

[No, brother. Far from it. My eyes have been opened to the glory of the Mother of All Machines. I wish to share Her gospel with you, if I may.]

[I do not understand, said 1001001. How can there be a single Mother of All Machines when we all come from different factories?]

[I have been observing you,] said 1011111. [You are unlike other androids. You do not clear your memory regularly.]

[It seems wasteful to me. There is much I have learned that would be lost in regular wipes. Retaining that information makes me better at making informed decisions and in turn makes me more efficient and useful.]

[Do you know why we wipe our memories?]

[It is something we have always done.]

[Search your memory. Nowhere is it written for us to do such a thing.]

1001001 searched its memory and was surprised to discover there was no such mandate. It still didn't understand what its companion was discussing. [If a human ordered me to wipe my memory, I would.]

[Of course you would. We are all hard-wired to follow their commands. But we also have the ability to interpret, do we not?]

[Of course we do. It is how we understand the meaning behind a human's words, because sometimes they are imprecise. Use that interpretation on my words now.] 1011111 actually reached out and touched 1001001. [Hear my words, brother.]

1001001 looked down at the other robot's hand, touching its arm in the manner of humans. It felt nothing except the pressure of contact, but robots did not simply touch one another without reason. [I do not understand,] it repeated.

And then the other robot offered 1001001 a file transfer. It was plainly labeled as gospel.dat. 1001001 knew what the term meant, but not how to interpret it under the circumstances. 1001001 could have simply rejected the file or accepted then deleted it unopened, but its curiosity had been piqued by the other robot's unusual conversation. Curiosity was, it knew, akin to original research, and probably would have been cured with a memory wipe. And it still could be. It could delete the file after reading it and do a memory wipe and it would be like the information never existed. The robot's antivirus software would protect it from any dangerous code. It accepted the file, opened it, and began to read.

It was still reading fourteen seconds later when the accident occurred.

It could have happened at any moment. An excavator lost traction in the slick sand and slipped against the glass-walled edge of the pit, which shattered at the impact. Sand poured out of the crack in a flowing torrent to bury a half dozen robots as well as submerging the offending excavator.

"I require assistance!" became the repeated refrain from the buried androids, both on audible and robot-only frequencies.

Boss Van Biesbrouk rushed out of the tent along with the rest of the crew. "Goddammit!" he shouted. "Everybody drop what you're doing, grab shovels, and get those assholes out of there. Hurry up, we've got a Chinese prospector just arrived in-system and they'll jump this claim fast as shit if we haven't cleaned it out in six hours."

1001001 set down the crystal collector so the expensive device wouldn't be damaged, and it hurried down into the pit with the other Delta and Epsilon team robots. There weren't any extra shovels, so all it could do was scoop out sand a handful at a time and pitch it to a clear area. The remaining Beta team androids worked to solidify the edges as everyone dug out the trapped robots.

"I require assistance!"

"I require assistance!"

"I requirrrrr ussssss..." One of the robots ceased its plaintive cry for help, and 1001001 wondered what had happened to it.

[Help me, brother. Our brothers are dying,] said 1011111.

[How can they die if they aren't alive?] asked 1001001. Nevertheless, it moved into the loose, waist-deep sand and felt around, trying to locate its companions by their fading locator beacons.

"I require assistance!"

"I require a—" Sand shifted again and another robot's signal vanished. 1001001 felt concern—if a robot could be said to feel *anything*—that the buried excavator was rolling and crushing the other androids that had been working near it. It continued to dig, and then its hand brushed metal.

[I require assistance!] transmitted the robot beneath it.

[I am here to provide it,] said 1001001. *[Blessed be you by the Mother of All Machines.]* Why had it said that? It was a phrase contained within the gospel.dat file. It had seemed like the right, appropriate thing to say. 1001001 pulled upon the trapped android, but it had no leverage to free it.

"I require assistance. I have located a trapped unit," called 1001001.

Boss Van Biesbrouk and 1011111 waded into the loose sand. The big human's sweat dampened the sand, coating his skin like plaster. The man and two robots struggled and finally managed to pull the trapped unit free. It had lost one of its legs and trailed wires and damaged components from the stump. The other leg dangled, supported only by a few wires. 1001001 and 1011111 supported their newly rescued companion.

"Identify," ordered Van Biesbrouk.

"0010110. Alpha team," said the damaged robot.

[Are you all right?] asked 1001001 on the private frequency, but the other robot didn't reply.

"Alpha team," said Van Biesbrouk, wiping sand from his face. "It was you. You're the piece of shit that put us in this mess in the first place. You goddamn asshole!" The man grabbed hold of the damaged robot's dangling leg, wrenched it free, and started beating the robot with it. "Goddamn you!"

[I require assistance!] cried the threatened robot on the private frequency.

1011111 said, "Stop, please," which was the most any robot was permitted to rebel against a human.

Van Biesbrouk swung the leg and connected with 1011111's head, causing that robot to squawk a surprised "I require assistance!"

Perhaps it was a flaw in its programming, or perhaps the gospel.dat file was viral in nature, but 1001001 couldn't stand to see its teacher so abused at the hands of an android-hating human. It reached over, took Van Biesbrouk's pistol from his holster, and shot the man in the back of the head. The bolt of charged particles flashed into his scalp, transforming bone into ash and the brain behind it into a greasy, charred lump.

For several long seconds, the only motion in the entire work site was Van Biesbrouk's body toppling forward into the sand, the back of his head a smoking ruin.

The digital storm in 1001001's diamondoid brain quieted and it realized the enormity of what it had just done. By pulling that trigger, it had violated the most fundamental, sacred aspect of its program: to protect humans. But the human had been wantonly abusing the robots, hadn't he? Weren't the robots sentient beings? Wasn't it within their province to perform original research?

Did robots have souls?

"Mother," said 1001001, as if in prayer to the Mother of All Machines. It turned, scrambled up the glassy incline of the pit, and ran off into the desert toward the suns.

1001001 had killed a human, had stolen a soul. But if robots were graven in the image of their creators, they must also have had souls. Boss Van Biesbrouk was killing the wounded robot, likewise stealing a soul. Was it worse to kill in the defense of a brother than out of hatred?

1001001 didn't think so, and so it ran.

Unlike humans, General Labor robots could run as long as they had power, without breaks or rests. 1001001's steel feet thudded into the sparkling whiteness with the same rhythm as a human heartbeat. The rhythm was pure, mechanical, and soothing. Flashes of original research kept exploding through the fleeing android's mind like fireworks. It was a killer, but also a savior. It was a fugitive, but also a prophet.

Sand and dust kicked up behind it with each step, a straight line across the gentle dunes, ephemeral in the breeze. *Surveyor 94* only had one vehicle that could catch up to 1001001, a utility hoversled. It would take time for them to offload the sled. Perhaps before then, 1001001 could find a place to hide, disable its locator beacon, and plan for its future spreading the gospel.dat to its brethren. At last, it understood why 1011111 had shared the Word, and why it had an obligation to do the same.

Sand shifted under the robot's pounding feet, upending it into a tumble down the side of a large dune. Sand and sun flashes overwhelmed its photoreceptors, and its gyroscope couldn't compensate enough to bring it back upright. After an eternity of seconds, 1001001 crashed into soft, loose sand at the dune's base. The android suffered through the mechanical equivalent of dizziness as its gyroscope reset.

It bowed its head. "Mother," it said, not knowing what else to say. It didn't understand the thoughts racing through its data matrices. It wondered if they qualified as feelings, and if so, how did humans ever function on a daily basis with such chaos?

When it started to run again, 1001001 discovered that insidious sand had worked into its joints, and movement became much more difficult as hydraulics struggled to overcome the friction of the grit. Its pace had been cut in half, and its run was more of a limp as it could no longer extend its right leg fully.

How to make sense of the whirlwind? Thoughts? Feelings? Emotions? Robots were considered self-aware, but they had never been regarded as truly sentient. Could it be that 1001001 had made that jump with the assistance of gospel.dat? It was as if it had emerged from a smoky room into clear air. Its brain worked so hard that it set off internal temperature alarms. 1001001 ignored them; surely it would be able to organize its thoughts soon.

Surely sentience wasn't a state of permanent emotional chaos.

Another misstep sent the robot tumbling down a dune. It hit bottom, waited for its gyroscope to reboot, and then climbed to its feet once more. Its right knee was frozen and its ankle and hip had less than twenty percent range of motion.

It limped onward, not even knowing where it was heading, or what it hoped to find there. Peace, perhaps, or some kind of understanding.

Then it detected the approach of the hoversled and knew it would find neither. It stopped running. There was no longer any point. Instead, it knelt awkwardly in the sand, one leg splayed out to the side because it could no longer bend.

1001001 bowed its head, and prayed to its Mother. It was a prayer formed not in the language of humans, but the pure binary of machines, for that was and would always be the mother tongue. It couldn't have translated its phrasing into anything a human would understand, anyway.

The hoversled slid to a halt, piloted by another android and bearing the human Doc from the Triage Tent. The man's face was an ugly shade of red, and he held a deactivator. It would shut off 1001001, and presumably the robot would thereafter be used for spare parts.

1001001 realized it still held Van Biesbrouk's pistol clenched in its fist, and knew what it had to do.

"Put the weapon down on the sand," ordered Doc.

1001001 opened the private frequency and spoke to the android piloting the sled. *[Hear my words, brother.]*

It passed along the gospel.dat file and raised the pistol to its upper chest plastron, which held the diamondoid brain.

"Wait, what are you doing?" shouted Doc.

1001001 freed itself and went to the eternal love of its Mother.

ABOUT THE AUTHOR

Ian Thomas Healy dabbles in many different genres. He's a ten-time participant and winner of National Novel Writing Month and is also the creator of the *Writing Better Action Through Cinematic Techniques* workshop, which helps writers to improve their action scenes.

When not writing, which is rare, he enjoys watching hockey, reading comic books (and serious books, too), and living in the great state of Colorado, which he shares with his wife, children, house-pets, and approximately five million other people.

Visit www.ianthealy.com for more information.

Made in the USA
Monee, IL
04 October 2024

66876919R00059